Killer Cocktail

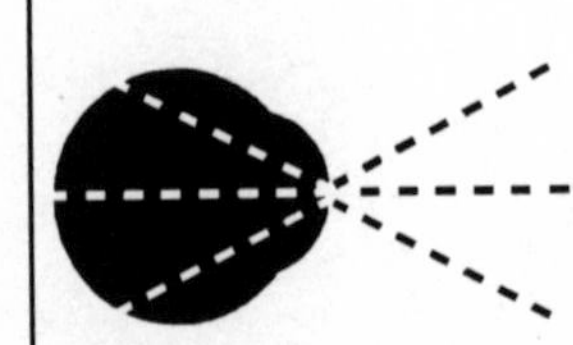

This Large Print Book carries the Seal of Approval of N.A.V.H.

A NIC & NIGEL MYSTERY

KILLER COCKTAIL

TRACY KIELY

THORNDIKE PRESS
A part of Gale, Cengage Learning

GALE
CENGAGE Learning

Farmington Hills, Mich • San Francisco • New York • Waterville, Maine
Meriden, Conn • Mason, Ohio • Chicago

GALE
CENGAGE Learning®

A Nic & Nigel Mystery.
Thorndike Press, a part of Gale, Cengage Learning.

This is a work of fiction. Names, characters, places, and incidents are either the product of the author's imagination or are used fictitiously, and any resemblance to actual persons, living or dead, business establishments, events, or locales is entirely coincidental.

Thorndike Press® Large Print Mystery.
The text of this Large Print edition is unabridged.
Other aspects of the book may vary from the original edition.
Set in 16 pt. Plantin.

LIBRARY OF CONGRESS CATALOGING-IN-PUBLICATION DATA

Names: Kiely, Tracy, author.
Title: Killer cocktail / by Tracy Kiely.
Description: Large print edition. | Waterville, Maine : Thorndike Press, 2016. | Series: A Nic & Nigel mystery | Series: Thorndike Press large print mystery
Identifiers: LCCN 2016025781 | ISBN 9781410492791 (hardcover) | ISBN 1410492796 (hardcover)
Subjects: LCSH: Hollywood (Los Angeles, Calif.)—Fiction. | Large type books. | GSAFD: Mystery fiction.
Classification: LCC PS3611.I4453 K55 2016b | DDC 813/.6—dc23
LC record available at https://lccn.loc.gov/2016025781

Published in 2016 by arrangement with Midnight Ink, an imprint of Llewellyn Publications, Woodbury, MN 55125-2989 USA

Printed in Mexico
1 2 3 4 5 6 7 20 19 18 17 16

To Barbara Kiely,
the best mother-in-law and nanny
anyone could ask for.

ACKNOWLEDGMENTS

I owe a big thank you to Aimee Hix and Mollie Cox Bryan for kindly telling me who my murderer was. I also want to thank my family for putting up with my panic attacks as my deadline grew near. I'd like to say that it will never happen again, but I think we all know that's a pipe dream. Also, thanks to Bridget Kiely and Barbara Poelle for talking me off the cliff from time to time (I've been advised to note that "time to time" roughly equals once a week). And finally, to everyone at Midnight Ink, especially Terri Bischoff — thank you for helping me bring Nic, Nigel, and Skippy to life.

Prologue

HNS! — Your Hollywood News Source

Melanie Summers Dead of Apparent Drug Overdose

By M. Reynolds* May 10, 1996

Melanie Summers, perhaps one of the most ambitious and beloved actresses of her generation, died on Thursday while filming the highly anticipated adaption of E. E. Berry's Pulitzer Prize–winning novel, *A Winter's Night.* She was 23.

The death, from an apparent drug overdose, was confirmed early this morning by law enforcement officials. Ms. Summers was found unresponsive in her trailer by her long-time assistant, Sara Taylor, after failing to report to the set.

Ms. Summers's battles with addiction over the past years were no secret. Earlier this year, she checked into a rehabilitation program for heroin addiction. "I really thought she'd beat it this time," said Ms. Taylor. "She was feeling really good about her future."

A doe-eyed brunette beauty with a lopsided smile, Melanie Summers stepped into the spotlight at the age of six, capturing audience's hearts in the holiday classic *A Miraculous Moment* (1979). A prolific child star, she went on to appear in no less than 11 films over the next ten years. At 17, she landed her breakout adult role as Jenny Davis, the devoted WWII girlfriend in *A Soldier's Letter Home.* She not only won an Oscar for the role, but she also won the heart of her handsome co-star, John Cummings. The two moved in together the following year and quickly became one of Hollywood's most glamorous and talked-about couples.

OFF-SCREEN DRAMA

Summers's private life earned her almost as much press as her professional one. She was rumored to have had numerous relationships — both public and secret — with her co-stars, colleagues, and other stars, even after moving in with Cummings. The constant spotlight of the paparazzi soon took its toll, and Summers's behavior both on and off the set became erratic. Her much publicized DWI arrest two years ago resulted in her first stint in rehab, and last year she and Cummings called it quits. “I will always love Melanie,” said Cummings at the time, “but she needs to focus on her health right now.” Despite these setbacks, Ms. Summers was nevertheless a favorite of both audiences and film producers, both of whom kept her in great demand. Six months ago, she had been tapped to play the lead in *A Winter’s Night* opposite Cummings. Director Barry Meagher released a statement saying, “The cast and crew are utterly heartbroken. At this time, we have no idea who will replace Melanie. In my mind, she is irreplaceable.”

ONE

I was standing on the red carpet amid a boisterous crowd of Oscar hopefuls when a familiar voice shouted out over the din, "Nicole! Nigel! Over here!" Turning, I spotted Mandy Reynolds. A stately blonde with a perpetual tan and a wide smile, Mandy was a correspondent for *HNS! Television.* Her shows routinely ranked among the station's highest rated due in equal parts to her engaging personality and glamorous wardrobe. For tonight's broadcast, she was wearing a sleek sheath of intricately beaded crimson. The silhouette hinted at shapely curves underneath; the plunging neckline and thigh-high slit confirmed them.

"You look stunning," I said once she pushed through the hoard of people and joined us.

"I look like a high-class hooker," she countered, as she kissed me on my cheek. "But in this industry a little bad taste is practically mandatory."

Nigel laughed. "According to Dorothy Parker, 'A little bad taste is like a nice dash of paprika.' "

"Which is why, were she alive today, she'd be my best friend," Mandy said. Glancing down at her crimson gown, she added, "However, I doubt even Dorothy would call this a dash. It's more of a dollop."

"In that case, she'd probably call you a dollop of a trollop," Nigel said.

"She would, wouldn't she?" Mandy agreed. "And then I'd get mad, and we wouldn't be friends anymore. I mean, let's be honest. The woman could be a bit bitchy at times."

"Maybe it's for the best that she's dead," said Nigel in a sympathetic voice.

Mandy laughed and then focused on the enormous dog seated regally at our feet. Large, even by bullmastiff standards, Skippy's fawn-colored head came just past my hip. In deference to the formality of the occasion, Nigel had secured a black silk bowtie around his thick neck.

"I can only assume that this creature belongs to you," she said.

Nigel nodded. "This is Skippy. He's new."

"That's one word for him," Mandy said. "Although I doubt it would be *my* first choice. Wherever did you get him?"

Draping his arm across my shoulders, Nigel pulled me close. "Well, Mandy," he began, his voice wistful, "sometimes when a man and a woman love each other very much . . ."

". . . the man drags a giant bullmastiff through a crowded bar and claims it followed him home," I finished.

"Only you would call a bar 'home,' Nigel," Mandy said shaking her head. "But, seriously? *Skippy* can't be his real name. He looks more like a Thor or a Zeus. Hell, even *Brian* would be more believable." She took a step closer, reaching out to scratch Skippy behind his ears. Skippy thumped his tail happily. "Does he know any tricks?" she asked.

"When he jiggles the martini shaker, Nigel comes running," I offered.

"Smart dog," Mandy said as she continued to play with Skippy's ears. "So, do you have time for a quick interview? My producer will skin me alive if I don't get the latest on those videos you found."

Nigel nodded his dark head. "Sure. You know I'm always happy to talk . . ."

"Oh, yes. I know how you love to talk," Mandy interrupted, pointing a manicured finger at his chest. "So, let's set some ground rules first, shall we? One, stick to the topic at hand. And two, *behave.*"

Nigel opened his blue eyes wide. *"Moi?"*

Mandy narrowed her own and leveled him with a hard stare. "Yes. *Vous.* Interviews with you are notoriously dangerous. Need I remind you of the time you recited a rather crude limerick about Oscar's genitalia — *on live TV*? If I remember correctly, you rhymed 'golden lord' with 'impotent gourd.' "

"Well, you have to admit . . ." Nigel began, but Mandy cut him off.

"And don't even get me started about that foul-mouthed and apparently *inebriated* parrot you had with you," she finished.

"Mandy, I swear, I had no idea that Roscoe even *knew* those words, let alone that he felt that way about you," Nigel said. "Besides, he was perfectly well behaved in the limo. How was I to know he couldn't hold his liquor?"

"There are so many things wrong with that question, Nigel, I don't know where to begin," Mandy said, "But, for my sake, please, *please* behave. I've been on a god-damn citrus cleanse for the last week and a half, and keeping up with you is hard enough on my best days."

"I'll be good," Nigel said, and then raised his two fingers and added, "Scout's honor."

"Oh, please," Mandy scoffed. "Unless the Scouts now give out badges for mixology, I'm not buying it. But I need this interview, so I'll just have to risk it." With a nod of her head, she turned and called to her cameraman. "Bob? Over here. We're going to do a quick interview."

A lanky man with a receding hairline and bushy beard nodded and walked toward us. "Ready when you are," he said, hoisting his camera onto his right shoulder.

"Okay," Mandy replied. "On three, two, one." The light from Bob's camera flashed on as Mandy squared her shoulders and raised her microphone. "Hello! This is Mandy Reynolds, and welcome back to the Academy Awards!" she beamed brightly at the camera before pivoting back to Nigel and me. "I'm here with the *always* charming Nicole and Nigel Martini. Nigel, of course, is the founder of Movie Magic, the company responsible for finding and restoring hundreds of films that were once thought lost forever. But what's really got Hollywood buzzing is his recent discovery of famed producer Frank Samuels's daughter's home videos from the set of the cult classic *A Winter's Night.* Now, Nigel, you just purchased Frank's former home. I understand that's where you found the videos, is that right?"

"That's right, Mandy," answered Nigel. "They were in the attic."

"The attic?" Mandy repeated in surprise.

Nigel nodded. "Yes, you see shortly after moving in, Nic and I were playing the game Never Ever Have I, and . . ."

"And we found the videos in the attic," I said quickly, giving Nigel's hand a warning squeeze.

Mandy's eyes widened briefly, and she moved on to her next question. "Have you been able to watch all the footage yet?"

"Not yet," answered Nigel, "but it's clear that Frank's daughter, Danielle, had a great deal of access on the set. She filmed the cast and crew while they ate, while they rehearsed, and while they discussed the story line. I think it's going to provide a rare glimpse into the filming process of one of America's favorite movies."

"Was Danielle able to capture any of Melanie Summers's work before she died?"

"A fair amount actually," Nigel answered.

"I'm curious to see how she interpreted the lead role of Hanna Gertchaw," said Mandy. "Of course, as we all know, Christina Franklin was initially cast to play Hanna's sister, Freda, in the film, and was given the lead after Melanie's untimely death. She won her first Oscar for that role."

"From what I've seen so far, I'd say that they had different interpretations of Hanna," said Nigel. "Melanie saw her as tougher and a little less tortured than how Christina ultimately portrayed her. It's intriguing to think how Melanie's interpretation might have affected the movie as a whole."

"Just utterly fascinating," Mandy said. "So, what are you doing with the videos now?"

"My staff and I are transferring them to our computers. Once that's done, we'll edit them into a cohesive narrative and release it."

"Any idea when that might be?" Mandy asked.

"We're hoping to have it ready for release by this summer," Nigel answered.

"Well, we'll all be looking forward to it," Mandy said, her tone indicating the interview was over. "Thanks again for stopping, and enjoy the show!" She smiled at the camera until the light went off. "We get what we need, Bob?" she asked.

"Got it," Bob answered as he lowered the camera from his shoulder.

"Great. Thanks, Nigel," said Mandy. "Promise me that you'll call when the footage is complete. I'd be happy to help you promote it. Not that you'll need it, of course. People are going to go nuts over any footage of Melanie." She paused and looked at him sideways. "Of course, all the old rumors are bound to surface again."

Nigel rolled his eyes. "You mean the one that claims Melanie faked her death to get away from it all?"

"Actually," she said, "I was thinking about the one that claims she was murdered."

Two

"*Both* theories are absurd," said Nigel.

"Why is it absurd to think that she faked her death?" Mandy asked.

"Because contrary to the Elvis sightings routinely documented in *The National Enquirer,* celebrities simply do not fake their deaths and then disappear into thin air," said Nigel.

"Some do," said Mandy. Turning to me, she asked, "What do you think, Nic? After all, you're the detective."

"Ex-detective," I corrected. "My days with the New York City Police Department are over."

"Fine. Then as *an ex-detective* what do you think?" she asked.

"I have to admit it's not something that keeps me up at night . . ." I said. Nigel opened his mouth to say something, but I quickly placed my hand over his mouth. "But, if pressed, I guess I'd have to ask why

Melanie would fake her death in the first place? She'd just landed one of the most sought-after roles in Hollywood. Her career was set to take off."

"True, but some believe her life was in danger from a stalker fan," said Mandy. "Others believed she had a fatal illness and wanted to die without the media attention. And then there are those who claim that she just got sick of Hollywood and wanted out."

"So, if she faked her death, then where did she go?" I asked. "In this day and age, it's kind of hard to live under the radar."

"I don't know," said Mandy. "But, I've heard theories ranging from she married an obscure European prince to that she's living on a beach in Tahiti."

"That in and of itself should give you a hint as to the collective IQ of these theorists," Nigel said as he removed my hand from his mouth. "But, even they're brighter than the 'She Was Murdered' theorists."

"Why? You have to admit, she wasn't very well liked," Mandy countered.

"By those standards, half of Hollywood would be dead," Nigel said. "And, I think that if Melanie were murdered, *someone* might have noticed. You know, like the coroner. Or her assistant. Or just about anyone on the set."

Mandy turned to me. "I'm sure Nic would agree with me that lots of murders go unreported."

"Not if I'm sober, I wouldn't."

"If that's a clever ploy to get me to buy you a drink," said Mandy with a grin, "then drinks are on me tonight."

Nigel shook his head. "No deal. There are some lines even *I* won't cross for a free drink."

"Fine," said Mandy, "but at least answer me this. Nic, you're a good judge of character." She winked at Nigel and added, "*Normally.* From what you've seen of the footage, what did you make of her?"

"She was a great actress," I said slowly. "And obviously, we haven't watched all of the footage yet, but, from what I've seen so far, I'd say she could be . . . difficult."

Mandy laughed. "If by 'difficult' you mean a spoiled brat with a rotten soul, then I'd agree with you."

"I was somewhat surprised," I admitted. "She was always portrayed as America's Sweetheart."

Mandy scoffed. "America's Sweetheart, my ass. That reputation was created by the studio's publicity machine, and even then it took a team of full-time workers to make it believable. The real Melanie Summers was a manipulative, egotistical little shit who only cared about herself." Mandy paused and then added, "May she rest in peace, of course."

"What a pretty eulogy that would have made," I said.

Mandy laughed. "Oh God, the stories I could tell. She was one of the first celebrities I was assigned to cover. On the outside, she was a beautiful girl with great talent. On the inside, she was poison. Pure poison."

Behind us a collective scream went up as the latest It Girl stepped onto the red carpet. An actress better known for her revealing outfits than her talent, she had outdone herself tonight. Her skirt was nothing more than a scrap of transparent gauze; however, this was rendered modest by the two bedazzled band-aides that served as a bodice. Mandy let out a small sigh. "Dear God, tits and no talent certainly are all the rage these days," she said with a small shake of her head.

"Now *that's* a dollop of a trollop," I said.

"That's not a dollop," Nigel protested. "That's a trough. And it makes me want to gouge out my eyes. Is that the reaction she wants?"

"Somehow, I doubt she's going for the

Oedipus Rex effect," I said.

"Somehow, I doubt she can *pronounce* Oedipus Rex," said Nigel.

"Well, it's my lucky job to feign interest in the half-dressed minx," Mandy said as she started to walk away. "I'll see you later at the Vanity Fair party, yes?"

"Absolutely," Nigel said with wave. "We'll be sitting at a table with Elvis."

Mandy's response was nonverbal, but nevertheless unambiguous. Nigel burst out laughing. "Roscoe would be so proud of you!" he yelled after her.

"Speaking of which," I asked him, "did you really rhyme 'golden lord' with 'impotent gourd'?

"Trust me," he said as he offered me his arm, "It was a vast improvement over what Roscoe suggested."

Three

Skippy did not go unnoticed by the rest of the press. As we continued along the red carpet, Nigel offered them various explanations as to his identity:

"It's a glandular issue. We try not to call attention to it."
"I happen to think my wife is a very attractive woman."
"He's playing Chewbacca in the upcoming Star Wars film. Picture him furrier. And with a dashing belt."
"What dog?"

At the entrance of the Dolby Theater, DeDee Evans, Nigel's latest hire to the company waited for us. While the organizers of the Oscars had allowed Skippy to accompany us on the red carpet, they drew the line at actually letting him inside the theater. Nigel's claim that Skippy was a service dog had not been entertained as even remotely serious.

"Hello, DeDee," Nigel said as he handed her Skippy's leash — or reins — depending on your viewpoint.

"Hello, Nigel. Nic," DeDee smiled broadly. "It's so exciting to be here!" DeDee was a small and wiry woman with a pronounced nose and square jaw. Up until a few years ago, she had been a housewife living in Tallahassee, Florida, with her husband, Reggie. She had been content to put aside her dream of becoming a movie critic so she could help Reggie run his plumbing business. That contentment changed to contempt when she discovered that Reggie offered additional services to his female clients — services that went far beyond unclogging stubborn drains. DeDee quickly filed for divorce, left Tallahassee, and moved to New York. Within three years, she'd obtained her masters in film studies. Six months later, she came to work for Nigel.

Petting Skippy's head, DeDee now said, "It's a shame that they wouldn't let you take Skippy inside. He looks so handsome."

"I know," said Nigel. "I don't understand why the Academy refused to accept that he's a service dog."

"Maybe because he isn't?" I offered.

Nigel shook his head. "But, *they* don't know that. Besides, I gave them a perfectly good reason for needing him tonight."

I laughed. "Nigel, please. You told them that you suffered from acute zelotypophobia."

"So?" he countered. "It's not as if it isn't a real thing."

DeDee pulled her eyebrows together. "Zeloty . . . what?" she repeated.

"A fear of jealousy," I explained.

DeDee let out a sharp bark of laughter. "Well, this would definitely be the place to trigger an attack."

"Thank you," Nigel said before turning to me as if validated. "That was my point *exactly.* As it is, I'm already starting to feel anxious."

"That's only because there's no bar out here," I said. "Try breathing out of your third eye or something until we get inside." Focusing back to DeDee, I said, "Thanks again for agreeing to watch Skippy tonight. I left his food out on the counter, but don't let him con you into having seconds. I also left you a dinner in the fridge. A word of advice, don't leave it unattended. Skippy's not above stealing other people's food. If he gets to be too much, put him in our room and turn on QVC. He loves it."

"Just don't let him order anything," warned Nigel. "He has terrible taste."

"We probably won't be back until very late," I continued. "The guest room is all set up for you. If you need anything, call." I gave Skippy a dubious stare. "No funny stuff, mister," I instructed.

Skippy wagged his tail and barked. My concerns were not mollified.

DeDee gave me a reassuring smile. "Don't worry about us, Nic. We'll be fine. I plan on working some more on the videos. They're really starting to come together."

"Well, don't work too hard. You're already doing us a huge favor," I replied. "The last time we left Skippy alone, he removed all of the wallpaper in the kitchen."

"And in under thirty minutes, too," Nigel added proudly.

"Nigel, it wasn't a good thing."

"You never liked that wallpaper to begin with," he argued. "Besides, it would have taken most contractors *triple* that time to do the job. Think of the money he saved us. If anything, he did us a favor."

I stared at him. "We are never having children," I said after a beat.

Nigel clasped his hands over Skippy's ears. "How can you say that in front of him, you heartless wench?" he whispered in mock horror. "Come here, Skippy," he said, reaching into his pocket, "Daddy's got some bacon for you. Mommy didn't mean it."

I rolled my eyes as Skippy wolfed down the bacon. "That better be all of it," I warned Nigel. "I don't care if you *do* look like a product of Oscar de la Renta; if you *smell* like a product of Oscar Mayer, I am *not* sitting with you."

DeDee laughed and said, "I'll keep an eye on Skippy. You two go have fun."

We patted Skippy good-bye one more time and took our place in a crowded line for the entrance. Within minutes, a slight man with a pockmarked face approached us. His dry, graying hair seemed to be combed in every direction. His posture was hunched. Grey eyes watched us from behind thick glasses. The laminated placard around his neck indicated he was a member of the press. His threadbare suit indicated that he wasn't a very successful one. "I heard you are Nigel Martini," he said. His voice was harsh and carried a faint accent I couldn't immediately place.

Nigel smiled affably. "You heard right," he said extending his hand. "And you are?"

"David Luiz, Hollywood Foreign Press," the man said, shaking Nigel's hand. He ran a pale tongue over his dry, cracked lips and turned his attention to me. "And this beautiful woman here must be Mrs. Martini," he said.

"Well, it would be damned awkward if she wasn't," Nigel said. "Now, how can I help you?"

"Those movie tapes," Mr. Luiz continued after an uncertain glance at me, "the ones with Melanie Summers? I represent someone who wants those tapes," he said, his voice low. He reached into his coat pocket, took out a business card, and handed it to Nigel. "I've been authorized to make you a very generous offer."

Nigel glanced at the card before shaking his head apologetically. "I'm sorry, Mr. Luiz," he said. "But, the tapes aren't for sale."

"I wouldn't be so hasty, Mr. Martini," he said, widening his smile and taking a step closer to Nigel. "You haven't even heard my offer yet."

"I don't need to," Nigel answered. "I'm not interested."

"My client will be very disappointed to hear that."

"I'll send flowers," said Nigel.

"I'm sorry, Mr. Martini," Mr. Luiz continued his voice growing anxious, "but I think you're being very foolish."

"You're not the first," Nigel admitted.

The line began to move. Nigel put his hand on the small of my back and began to guide me forward. "Now, if you'll excuse me, Mr. Luiz," he said, "I need to get some air."

Mr. Luiz regarded Nigel with a puzzled stare. "But, there's air out here," he protested.

"True," agreed Nigel, "but I need gin in my air. Good night, Mr. Luiz."

Footage from the Set of *A Winter's Night* 5/4/96

Train Station Set in Post WWII Germany

Actors in period costume stand along the track. The camera pans over rather shakily and then stops on Johnny Cummings, a handsome young man about 24 years old, dressed in a WWII American soldier's uniform for his role as Donny. He is tall with dark hair and green eyes. He is standing in front of a lovely young woman of about the same age. She is Melanie Summers, who plays the role of Hanna. She has dark hair and large blue eyes. Her braided hair forms a wreath around her head. She wears a frayed dress of faded gingham. She looks up at him with sad eyes.

JOHN/DONNY (gently) Hanna, please don't look at me like that. You know that I have to leave. But I promise you, I will send for you as soon as I can.

MELANIE/HANNA I know, Donny. I do

believe you. It's just hard to see you go. I . . . I love you, Donny.

JOHN/DONNY (pulling her into his arms) I love you, too. It's only for a little while. Don't you know that I'd move heaven and earth to keep us together? You're my forever.

John leans down and kisses Melanie, but suddenly grimaces and pulls back.

JOHN (no longer in character) Jesus!

A voice off camera suddenly yells, "CUT!" The camera swings toward the voice. It is the director, Barry Meagher, a tall man with messy black hair. He runs his hand through it making it even worse. He pushes his glasses up on his head and closes his eyes in frustration.

BARRY What the hell is wrong now?

JOHN (outraged) She bit me!

MELANIE (indignant) Well, next time don't jam your tongue down my throat!

JOHN Jam my . . . ? Are you crazy? You're intentionally trying to sabotage my scenes.

MELANIE Why in the name of God, would I do that?

JOHN (quietly) Because you're a mess. Because you're a mess, and you've lost your touch, and everyone knows it.

Melanie reacts as if she were slapped. John looks momentarily sorry for his words.

BARRY (interrupting) Enough! Would you two please just cut the crap so we can shoot the damn movie? You're wasting everyone's time, but more importantly, you're wasting *my* time. I swear to God, if you two don't get your shit together fast, I'll have you *both* tossed off this movie! Got it?
MELANIE Got it. Sorry, Barry.
JOHN Ready. Sorry.

Various crew members recheck the lighting and the actors take their positions. Barry returns his glasses to his eyes and steps behind a large camera.

BARRY All right. Let's try again. ACTION!
JOHN/DONNY (gently) Hanna, please don't look at me like that. You know that I have to leave. But I promise you, I will send for you as soon as I can.
MELANIE/HANNA I know, Donny. I do believe you. It's just hard to see you go. I . . . I love you, Donny.
JOHN/DONNY (pulling her into his arms) I

love you, too. It's only for a little while. Don't you know that I'd move heaven and earth to keep us together? You're my forever.

John gently cups Melanie's face, and they stare at one another for a long moment. John slowly moves to kiss her. His arm snakes around Melanie's waist, pulling her closer. After a beat, Melanie arches into John, wrapping her arms around his neck.

BARRY Cut! That was perfect! Great job everyone. Okay, let's break for lunch.

The set empties as everyone heads for the craft table. John pulls his head back. Melanie quickly removes her arms from John's neck and steps away, keeping her head down. John begins to walk away as well, but then Melanie calls to him.

MELANIE John? Do you have a second? I need to talk to you about something.

John stops, and turns. His expression is wary.

JOHN I'm not up for any more drama right now, Melanie.

MELANIE Just shut up for a second, will

you? This is important.

JOHN Fine. Talk. But make it fast. I'm meeting someone for lunch.

MELANIE Who? Christina?

JOHN Actually, that's none of your business. Not anymore. Now what do you need to talk to me about?

MELANIE It's about what happened when we were in Cabo last month.

JOHN (frowning) Okay.

MELANIE Well, there's something you should know . . . (Her voice drops and her words are inaudible.)

John stares at Melanie. His expression grows angry but he says nothing.

A WOMAN'S VOICE (far off) Danielle? Danielle, honey? Where are you? It's time for lunch.

DANIELLE Coming, Mom!

The camera swings suddenly sideways, revealing a young woman of about twenty years old standing half in the shadows. She is petite with long auburn hair. It is Christina Franklin. She is staring intently at John and Melanie. The camera swings one more time to the floor and then goes dark.

Four

Almost an hour later, the theater lights dimmed, and the orchestra began to play. Attendees settled into their seats. Ushers signaled for quiet. Cameramen readied themselves. From above, a disembodied voice called out, "Live from the Dolby Theater, it's the Oscars! Ladies and Gentlemen, please welcome your host, Ellen DeGeneres!"

Wearing a fitted velvet tuxedo, Ellen strode across the stage. With a merry smile she greeted the cheering crowd in the auditorium. "Thank you!" she said. "Thank you very much. Before we get started, I want to say that you should think of yourselves as winners." She paused. "Not everyone, but all of you that have won before should."

The crowd laughed and settled in for the show. An hour later, the lull of the shorts, documentaries, and technical categories had taken its toll. Nigel was slumped low in his seat, his eyes at half-mast. My attempts to rouse him were ignored. When the Oscar for Best Actress was about to be announced, I gave him one last nudge. "Nigel! Wake up!" I hissed.

Nigel peeled one eye open and asked, "Is it over yet?"

"No, but they are about to announce Best Actress. Don't you want to watch?"

"You watch for me and tell me what happens," he said, closing his eye again.

I poked him again. "Why did you bother to come if you don't even watch?"

Nigel crossed his arms across his chest, his eyes still closed. "Because, *someone* told me there was an open bar this year."

"You really need to let that go. I said I was sorry."

"And I told you that I'm sleeping. Now, stop talking. You're interrupting me."

I gave up and focused again on the show. Anne Hathaway and Steve Carell were bantering as they read the nominees.

Among this year's candidates was Christina Franklin, the actress who ultimately portrayed the lead in *A Winter's Night.* Christina won her first Oscar for that role. In her acceptance speech, she called the win a bittersweet one and tearfully dedicated it to Melanie's memory. In the years after, she won three more Oscars and always spoke fondly of Melanie. Tonight she was up for her role in the movie *The Morning Came Early.* Her portrayal of a French seamstress trying to help Jews escape a Germany-occupied France during World War II had been universally praised by the critics and was a crowd favorite to win.

"And the winner is . . ." Anne Hathaway paused to open the envelope. After a quick glance, she happily called out, "Christina Franklin!"

The crowd burst into enthusiastic applause. Even the other nominees appeared genuinely happy for her. I pointed this out to Nigel, but he only kept his eyes closed and said, "They weren't nominated for Best Actress for nothing."

Christina gracefully made her way to the podium, stopping to hug a few friends on the way. The lights reflected off the silver beading of her gown, shimmering across every dip and curve. Making her way onto the stage, she humbly accepted the statue, and then turned to face the audience. In many ways there was little difference between the nineteen-year-old-girl who first rose to this podium twenty years earlier and the thirty-nine-year-old woman who stood here now. She was tall and lithe. Although it was pulled back tonight, her hair was as it had always been; a tawny mane of riotous curls. Her waiflike face was still youthful. Her enormous green eyes, famous for their ability to subtly convey a gamut of emotions, now sparkled joyfully.

"Thank you so much for this," she said in a soft voice, tilting her head to indicate the golden statue. Appearing for a moment at a loss for words, she reached up to smooth her hair before continuing. "There are so many people who made this possible," she said. "First, I want to thank my agent, Barbara Pooler, who convinced me to take this role. She is simply a force of nature. I suspect I will be hearing 'I told you so,' for a very long time." The audience laughed. "And, of course," Christina continued, "many thanks to the entire cast and crew of *The Morning Came Early.* You made the entire experience a wonderful one. To our director, Barry Meagher. Barry, where are you?" She sought him out in the crowd, her face softening when she found him. Barry Meagher was a tall, thin man with thick silver hair. His intense black eyes peered out at the world from under absurdly bushy eyebrows. A smile now split his craggy face, and he blew her an extravagant kiss. Christina grinned, pretended to catch it and blow it back. "Barry, it was truly a joy to work with you again," she said. "You must be my good luck charm. I won my first Oscar working with you on *A Winter's Night.* You always bring out the best in us. Without you, this never would have happened," she added gesturing to the Oscar. "And I hope you are called up here in a little bit to get yours for Best Director." She glanced around the room and, with a sly wink, quickly added, "No offense meant to the other nominees, of course." The crowed laughed good-naturedly. Christina paused and took a deep breath. "Finally, I'd like to thank my co-star and old friend, John Cummings."

There was a faint gasp from the audience. Next to me, Nigel opened his eyes and sat up in his seat. "Well, this should be good," he whispered.

Fastening her eyes on John, Christina continued, her voice soft. "Lord knows we've had our ups and downs, John, but I want you to know that I think you are one of the best actors out there today. You make everyone around you look good. I feel truly blessed to have been able to work with you again."

Around us, people craned their necks to gage not only John's reaction to this speech, but also that of the young woman's sitting next to him.

Neither disappointed.

John's eyes locked on Christina's with an expression of pride tinged with sadness. He bowed his dark head in acknowledgement of Christina's words before he, like their director, blew her a kiss. His gesture, however, had a far more intimate feel. As before, Christina pretended to catch the kiss. However, this time she did not return it. Instead, she balled her hand into a fist and held it close to her chest. "I think I'll hang on to this one for old time's sake," she said with a small smile.

The reaction of the woman next to John, Jules Dixon, was Hollywood drama at its finest. Her full, pink lips stretched into a tight smile across her round, kewpie doll face. Grabbing John's hand, she gave it a tight squeeze before leaning over into his seat and placing a possessive kiss on his cheek. John barely acknowledged the gesture. His gaze remained locked on Christina's.

From the podium, Christina gently kissed her still-balled hand before smiling her thanks again to the crowd and gracefully making her way off stage.

"Now, *that* is what I call great acting,"

said Nigel with a grin.

I looked over to where John and Jules sat. His face was unreadable. The same could not be said for Jules. She stared straight ahead, her eyes bright with anger; the brittle smile on her face fooling no one.

FIVE

After that, conversation mainly focused on rehashing the sordid details of the love triangle that was Christina, John, and Jules. "It's clear that she still loves him," announced a woman sheathed in a black silk gown seated behind me. "Despite his horrible behavior, she still loves him."

Her companion disagreed. "Oh, Dotty, how can you say that?" she chastised as she adjusted the strap of her gold dress. "After all their years together, he goes and gets that girl pregnant! Why, she's almost twenty years younger than he is! There is no way Christina still loves him. She's too smart for that."

Sometime after that, the man in front of us groused, "I don't see what the big deal is. John and Christina had been together for what — twenty years? The relationship had obviously run its course, and he found somebody new. It happens all the time."

"It hadn't run its course, you idiot," his wife hissed at him. "After Jules held that ridiculous press conference — from her hospital room, no less — announcing that the baby was John's, Christina made him do the right thing and marry her. He doesn't love Jules anymore than I love the way you suck your teeth, which by-the-way, is absolutely disgusting."

Later, a woman to my left wearing a pink trumpet gown, said, "I never understood why Barry Meagher ever cast Jules Dixon in *The Morning Came Early* in the first place. The only thing that girl knows how to do is take off her clothes and pout. The very idea of her playing a studious Jewish girl trying to save her family from the Nazis is ludicrous!"

"I know," agreed her date. "I can't image what the movie would have been like had she not gotten pregnant and dropped out. I keep picturing her trying to do a striptease with a snood."

In the ladies' room, a woman reapplying lipstick in the mirror sniffed smugly and said, "Well, that's what happens when you put career first. Christina and John never had any kids because she was more concerned with making movies than making babies."

"How do you figure that?" her friend demanded as she fluffed her blonde hair. "John met Jules while the three of them were filming *The Morning Came Early.* Why would you think that if Christina was home with a baby the affair wouldn't have happened?"

In the lobby, a balding man with a well-developed paunch said to his equally rotund friend, "I don't care if Jules Dixon can't act her way out of a paper bag. With a body like that, she doesn't need to. I mean, Christina's still good-looking and all, but let's face it, she's pushing forty. Let me tell you, once they hit that age, it's all downhill."

"John Cummings is one lucky son-of-a-bitch," his friend agreed as he tossed back the rest of his scotch. "Hell, I wouldn't say no to a fling with Jules Dixon, even if it meant being hit with a palimony suit."

Two women who, based on their disgusted expressions, I guessed to be their wives returned from the restroom in time to hear this. The taller of the two jabbed a lethally manicured finger into the soft spot of the first man's stomach. "Oh, is that true, Mr. I-Wheeze-if-I-Have-to-Go-Up-a-Flight-of-Stairs? And you think *you're* some prize? Did someone forget to tell me that perpetual upper lip sweat is all the rage?"

"I'm just curious how you think you could even *get* someone like Jules Dixon, let alone get her pregnant, when you need Viagra just to go to the bathroom?" the second woman scoffed at the scotch drinker.

"Well, if you ask me, Jules Dixon is a no-class, piece-of-work," said another woman at the bar, her arms crossed tightly across her ample chest. "Did you read where she said Johnny had never been happy with Christina, and that their relationship was all a ploy by the publicity department? Not once has either Johnny or Christina said one mean word about the other to the press since their split. But apparently Jules didn't get a copy of the 'We're Going to Act Like Adults' memo. She's unbelievable. I mean, really, can you believe her?"

"For the last time, Martha, I have no idea who you are talking about nor do I care to," replied her weary husband. "Now do you want a damn drink or not?"

Footage from the Set of *A Winter's Night* 5/2/96

The scene is a 1940s nightclub. John and Melanie sit at a table near a dance floor. Around them the film crew bustles about preparing the scene. John and Melanie sit in silence ignoring one another. Just off to the right Barry sits in his director's chair reading notes. A trim blonde with a forced smile approaches him. It is Janice Franklin, Christina's mother.

JANICE Barry! There you are. I've been looking everywhere for you.
BARRY (not looking up) How perceptive of you to think to look for me here. Your detractors clearly have underestimated you.
JANICE (smile slips) You're such a teaser.
BARRY (still not looking up) I've been called many things, Janice. Thankfully, that has never been one of them. (Finally looks up and pushes his reading glasses

on his head) What do you want, Janice?

JANICE Well, it's about Christina.

BARRY Imagine my surprise.

JANICE Yes, well, I wanted to talk to you about the Kitchen Scene. The one where Christina receives the break-up letter from her boyfriend? And then she breaks down and cries at the table?

BARRY (sighing) I'm familiar with the scene, Janice. What about it?

JANICE Well, I just heard that it's being cut. Is this true?

BARRY It is. The movie is going to run long as it is. I've got to trim the excess.

JANCIE But that's one of Christina's best scenes! And it's her only solo scene!

BARRY I'm aware of that, Janice. Unfortunately, we can't keep every scene or we are going to end up with a five-hour movie.

JANICE So, cut something else! What about that scene with Melanie in the tub? I don't see why we need that. She barely says a word in it.

BARRY (incredulous) I'm sorry. Did you really just suggest that I cut the scene in which the main character contemplates killing herself? The scene that is basically the turning point of the whole movie?

JANICE (crossing her arms over her chest)

I just think it's a little over done, that's all. I'm sure you could get across the point without taking up so much screen time. It's five minutes long, for Christ's sake! I know it's Melanie we're talking about here, but surely even she's capable of appearing to make a decision in a shorter amount of time.

BARRY (rubbing his eyes wearily) Please go away, Janice. I'm barely holding on by a thread as it is today. I simply can't deal with your crazy right now.

JANICE (angrily) My . . . my . . . *what?* Did you just call *me* crazy? *Me?* I'm not the one who is turning this movie into a one-woman showcase for Melanie Summers! Last time I checked, this movie was about a family's struggles — not just one girl's perpetual navel gazing!

BARRY It is a movie about a family, but the main character of that family — and the catalyst for most of the story — is Hanna. And I know you don't like this, but Melanie got the role of Hanna. Not Christina. So, unless you have something meaningful to say — which I grant you would be a first — I'd prefer it if you'd shut the hell up and let me direct my movie!

JANICE (not moving) What the hell is going on here, Barry? Ever since we've started shooting, you've changed the focus of this film. It's all about Melanie. I get that she's the star, but she's not the only character. And yet every day, you cut another scene so you can make one of hers longer.

BARRY (putting his glasses back on and reading his notes again) Once again, I have no idea what you're talking about, Janice.

JANICE Oh, I think you do. There's something rotten going on around here. And I intend to find out what it is.

Janice turns and storms away. After a moment, Barry pushes his glasses back onto his head and frowns at her retreating form.

Six

The after parties at the Oscars are a glitzier version of the high school bashes depicted in a John Hughes film; only the cool, rich kids are invited and even once inside those gilded walls, cliques still abound. The pinnacle of all these parties is, of course, the iconic gala hosted by *Vanity Fair.* Here the famous, the powerful, and the beautiful (and more often than not, a combination of all three) gather to gossip, celebrate, and network.

Nigel and I pushed our way past the throngs of press parked along Sunset Strip and presented our invitation to the alarmingly large, albeit polite, doorman. After he verified its authenticity, we were granted entry past the barricades and into the privileged sanctum beyond. My years on the force had left me more than a little cynical, but even I found myself starstruck at the scene before me. Here was Hollywood's elite, encircling me in a heady blur of expensive tuxedos, sequined gowns, false eyelashes, and tanned skin. As a variety of oldies songs played from hidden speakers, they mingled and congratulated one another all while scarfing down a seemingly never-ending supply of cocktails and cheeseburgers. The polite composure on display during the ceremony had been replaced with one far more casual. Shoes were removed; golden statues were employed as microphones, and outbursts of dancing were neither infrequent nor frowned upon.

Orbiting this celestial constellation was a steady stream of glam cigarette girls who cheerfully dispensed candy and e-cigarettes, the later being the only indication that we hadn't fallen through a wormhole and traveled back in time.

Nigel quickly snagged two flutes of champagne, and we made our way farther into the room. In one corner, I saw Steven Spielberg chatting with Tom Hanks and Rita Wilson. In another, Robert De Niro shared a joke with Ben Stiller. It was hard not to stare.

As Nigel and I helped ourselves to the complimentary cheeseburgers, Mandy approached us with a wide smile. The microphone she held earlier had been replaced with an e-cigarette. In her other hand was a glass of wine.

"Since when did you start smoking?" I asked her as she drew closer.

"About five minutes after the show ended," she said. "That goddamn juice cleanse was like having a weeklong colonoscopy. I feel like I have to counteract it with a few weeks of really bad habits."

"I don't see why people have such a hard time with juice cleanses," Nigel said. "I think they're pretty easy."

"Nigel," I said with a shake of my head, "for the hundredth time, cranberry juice and vodka do *not* constitute a juice cleanse."

Mandy gave a lusty sigh. "God, but wouldn't it be great if it did?" She took another puff of her cigarette and asked, "So, what did you think of the show?"

"It was a little long," Nigel and I said in unison.

Mandy rolled her eyes in agreement. "When is it not? That should be its tag line 'The Oscars — It's a Little Long.' "

I quickly pressed my finger over Nigel's mouth and turned to Mandy. "What about you?" I asked as Nigel laughed. "Were you happy with it?"

Mandy nodded and took a deep puff of her cigarette. "I got my interviews, and it ended on time. That's all I ever really care about. Of course, all anyone can really talk about is Christina's acceptance speech," said Mandy. "Speaking of which, what did you make of it?" she asked, her eyes bright.

"Pretty gracious, all things considered," I said.

Mandy gave an unlady-like snort. "Are you sure you used to be a detective?" she teased. "Because, if you ask me, it was payback tied up in a pretty gold bow. Karma is a bitch, and Christina just gave it John's address."

"How so?" Nigel asked.

Mandy took a puff of her cigarette. "Because Christina managed to plant the idea in Jules's tiny brain that things aren't over between her and John."

"Why do you say that?" I asked.

"Jules is in a royal snit," said Mandy. "Not that *that* is anything new, of course. Jules Dixon has never been one to hide her emotions. Unless," she added archly, "she's in front of a camera." She then tilted her chin toward the back of the room. "The 'happy couple' is over there," she said. "If you look closely, you'll note that Jules is trying not to appear like she wants to throw her drink in his face, and John is surreptitiously collecting napkins in case she does."

I glanced to where Mandy indicated. Jules and John were in the far corner of the room. They did not touch one another. They did not speak to one another. Eye contact was apparently also taboo.

"They don't exactly radiate joy, do they?" I said.

"Nope, they sure don't," Mandy responded with a grin.

I glanced at her. "You certainly seem to be getting a kick out of this. Why?"

Mandy shrugged. "No reason, really. I just don't get the fascination with Jules."

I made a rude noise. "You don't get the fascination with a twenty-something-year-old who has the body of a lingerie model and who was once described by an ex as being 'a sexual ninja in bed'?" I asked. "Seriously?"

"Back up," Nigel said, holding up his hand. "A sexual *ninja*? Is that good or bad?"

"Good," Mandy and I answered in unison.

"Really?" he asked, his expression unconvinced. "I mean, to each his own and all that, but it sounds more risky than risqué. Those nunchucks can be deadly. Especially in the wrong hands."

"That could be said about a lot of things," I said.

"You do have a point there," Nigel said.

"In fact, it reminds me of a girl I once heard of who . . ."

"I just don't think John should get his happily ever after," Mandy said interrupting. "Christina is a sweetheart, and she was devoted to John. I hate it when the men in this town think it's okay to trade in for the newer model. It's pathetic." She turned to Nigel for support. "*You* wouldn't leave Nic and marry a younger woman, would you?"

"Of course not," he replied, his tone appalled. Taking a sip of champagne, he added, "Do you have any idea how much weddings cost these days? It's obscene."

"Mother always said to marry a man with good financial sense," I confided happily to Mandy as I linked my arm through Nigel's.

Footage from the Set of *A Winter's Tale* *5/6/96*

Two stunt men walk through the moves of the fight that is to take place in a dancehall. Mattresses are placed on the floor for the actors to land on and chairs that easily break are placed in the appropriate spots. The men slowly circle each other, alternately jabbing and ducking, turning the violence into a slow dance. The camera stays on them, but voices can be heard nearby. One is raised in anger. It is the voice of Melanie Summers. The other voice is muffled.

MELANIE Are you serious? You can't be serious!

VOICE I'm sorry.

MELANIE You're sorry? You're *sorry*?

VOICE Of course, I am. I don't like this any more than you do. But we have to be pragmatic about this.

MELANIE Pragmatic? Did you just tell me that I have to be *pragmatic*?

VOICE No, I said *we* have to be pragmatic. I'm not going anywhere. But this . . . this can't happen. Not now.

MELANIE (laughing) Well, it's a bit late to decide that, don't you think? Because, news flash! It already did.

VOICE (calmly) I know that, but it's also something that can be easily undone.

MELANIE Easy for who precisely?

VOICE Easy was the wrong word. But you can't tell me that you really want this. This movie is going to be epic! It will make us!

MELANIE Oh, so now there is an "us" again. Funny how that word comes and goes. Just like you.

VOICE That's not fair.

MELANIE I'll tell you what's not fair! Not fair is being lied to. Not fair is being told that you matter when you don't. Not fair is being told that you have a future when you were just a fun time.

VOICE That's not what you are . . .

MELANIE You're a goddamn liar! You said it was over with her! You said you wanted to be with me! You said you would be with me! You promised me!

VOICE I never promised you . . .

MELANIE You did. (sounds of crying) You did, you bastard. You promised, you bastard, and I trusted you!

VOICE Melly, shhh . . . keep your voice down. I do want to be with you. I just can't right now. Surely you have to understand that.

MELANIE Oh, I understand perfectly! And soon everyone else will too.

VOICE What's that supposed to mean?

MELANIE It means I'm done. I'm done lying. And I'm done with you.

Seven

"Let me introduce you to Christina," said Mandy. "You'll love her."

I glanced over to where Christina sat. A few tendrils of her titian hair had escaped her chignon and now fanned out around her face. Her checks were flushed and her eyes were bright, either from the gold statue on the table before her or the martini glass beside it.

To one side of Christina, sat her twin brother, Sebastian. Although obviously not identical, there were some discernible similarities. They shared the same auburn hair and wide green eyes, high cheekbones, and taste in men. But whereas Christina was known for her reserved nature, Sebastian was just the opposite. He never met a microphone or camera that he didn't like, and as such was something of a darling of the tabloids. His long frame was sprawled in his chair, his right ankle resting on his left knee, and his left arm slung causally around the back of Christina's chair. With his right hand, he idly drummed out a rhythm on the linen tablecloth.

To Christina's other side was a woman I didn't recognize. Her blonde hair was arranged in a kind of puffy helmet. Her dress brought to mind a gruesome crime scene; blood red and seeming to go on forever. I guessed her to be about sixty-five, although I suspected that she'd punch me in the mouth if I actually said that out loud. Her skin had been pulled, her eyes had been lifted, and her lips had been plumped. The end result was a face that not only appeared to be at the mercy of a powerful g-force, but one that was also — and understandably — startled by the sensation.

"Who's that next to Christina?" I asked as we made our way to the table.

Mandy's lips twisted into a faint sneer. "That's Janice Franklin. Christina's mother."

"I take it you're not a fan?"

"Hardly," she replied. "The woman is toxic. She's done nothing but pimp out Christina since she was six months old. Christina didn't have a childhood; she had a job."

"Not exactly a unique story in this town,"

I observed.

"True. But we all thought that one day Christina would come to her senses and get rid of her. But Janice still serves as her manager, publicist, and, no doubt, her accountant," she said.

"Well, she *is* her mother," I offered.

"She's a bitch," Mandy corrected.

I shrugged. "No one ever said the terms were exclusive."

"What about Christina's father?" Nigel asked. "Is he in the picture?"

Mandy shook her head. "No, and from the way Janice tells it, he never was."

"So, it was an Immaculate Conception?" I asked, laughing. "Wow. You certainly don't hear of too many of *those* these days."

"That's not true," countered Nigel. "It happened to a cousin of mine." He paused. "And now that I think about it, a few girls in high school."

"Don't be an ass," said Mandy. "I just meant that he's not a factor in their lives. I don't know anything about him. No one does."

Christina jumped to her feet when she saw Mandy approaching. Opening her arms wide, she cried out excitedly, "Mandy! Can you believe it? I actually won!"

Mandy laughed and walked to her, hugging her tight. "I told you you would," she said.

"I honestly didn't think I had a chance this year," Christina said. "I really thought they were going to give it to Meryl."

Mandy stepped back and playfully poked Christina in her shoulder. "Nonsense," Mandy said. "I knew you had it sewn up the minute I saw that movie. You're always surprised when you win, which is one of the many reasons I adore you. Now, I know you haven't had a moment's bit of peace tonight, but I wanted to introduce some friends of mine." Turning to us, she said, "Christina, this is Nicole and Nigel Martini. They're the couple that bought Frank's old place and found the videos."

At the sound of our names, Sebastian's fingers ceased tapping, and Janice's head turned in our direction as if pulled by some unseen chord. Christina gave us a bright smile. "How lovely! I was hoping to meet you tonight. Won't you please join us?" she asked.

We said we would, and introductions were made. As we took our seats at the table, Sebastian deftly relieved a passing waitress of her tray of champagne cocktails and passed them around. I had just taken a sip of mine when Janice turned to me with a predatory smile. "I'm dying to hear all about these videos," she said. "Where did you find them?"

"Boxed up in the attic along with some old Christmas decorations," I explained. "They've just been collecting dust for the past twenty years. It's lucky we checked them. They could have just as easily been tossed out."

"Twenty years," Christina repeated with a sigh. "God, sometimes it feels just like yesterday. Well, until I look in the mirror that is," she added with a wry laugh.

"Oh, shut up," Mandy scoffed, "You've hardly aged a bit. Honestly, I don't know how you do it."

"It's the olive oil," Janice said. When we looked at her blankly, she continued. "My mother swore by its benefits for the skin," she explained. "She called it 'youth in a bottle.' "

"I thought that's what she called the scotch," said Sebastian, his brows pulled confusion.

Janice shot him a censorious look. "Your Nana did no such thing," she admonished.

"Well, *mine* certainly did," said Nigel. "For a moment, I thought we might be related."

Sebastian threw his head back and

laughed. It was the same rich tenor as his sister's. "Oh, I think I'm going to like you," he said.

Janice shot her son a quelling look before turning back to me. "So, have you watched them all yet?" she asked. "Danielle's videos, I mean."

"No," I answered, "It's going to take some time to get through them all, of course, but we're making progress. I'm looking forward to meeting Danielle. I've only spoken to her on the phone, but she said she and Frank would be here tonight."

"I think I remember her," said Sebastian slowly. Looking at Christina, he asked, "She was a little wisp of a thing, right? Long black hair; wore glasses?"

"That was Danielle," said Christina nodding. "She was so shy. I don't think I ever heard her say more than two words at a time. She reminded me of a little mouse; half the time you didn't even realize she was there. But, she's all grown up now. She recently started working for Frank, actually."

"Looks just like him too," said Janice. "It's a shame, really because her mother, Zelda, was gorgeous."

"She recently died, didn't she?" asked Sebastian.

"Just last year," Mandy said with a nod.

"Wasn't she living in Italy?" he asked.

"In Bellagio. She moved back there after her and Frank's divorce," Mandy answered. "Zelda never really liked Hollywood to begin with. She only came here because of Frank."

"Oh, that's right," said Christina. "Didn't he discover her on a beach somewhere?"

"Yes," confirmed Mandy. "In Camogli, on the Italian Riviera."

"Was she an actress there?" asked Nigel.

Mandy grinned at him. "No, she was topless there."

Nigel turned to me with an impish look in his eyes. "You know what I'm thinking we should do?" he asked.

"Yes," I answered. "But we're not."

Footage from the Set of *A Winter's Night* 5/2/96

Melanie Summers and Christina Franklin sit while makeup technicians apply their makeup. Christina focuses on reading the script on her lap. Melanie watches Christina in the mirror.

MELANIE Sorry to hear that your kitchen scene got pulled.

CHRISTINA (nods without looking up) Yeah. Me too.

MELANIE You were pretty good in it, I thought.

CHRISTINA Thanks.

MELANIE I wouldn't take it personally. That kind of thing happens all the time.

CHRISTINA (still not looking up) I'm sure it does.

MELANIE You still have the scene in the bedroom though, right?

CHRISTINA (her hand pauses on the script and she finally glances up) As far as I know.

MELANIE (smiling) Well, that's good. So, I understand you're seeing Johnny now, is that right?

CHRISTINA (warily) That's right.

MELANIE How's it going?

CHRISTINA Fine.

MELANIE That's good. He seems pretty smitten.

CHRISTINA (awkwardly) I . . .

MELANIE It's funny. Johnny and I were together for so long, I think people assumed that we would get back together someday. I certainly did. But I'm happy for you both. Just ignore all the crap people are saying.

CHRISTINA I wasn't aware that anyone was saying anything.

MELANIE (scoffs) Oh, sweetie, in this town, someone is always saying something.

Melanie looks at herself in the mirror. She fluffs her hair and then stands up.

MELANIE Well, I'm done here. I'll keep my fingers crossed that you get to keep your bedroom scene.

CHRISTINA (faintly smiling) Okay. Thanks.

Melanie turns and waves her hand over her shoulder as she walks away. Christina stares at her retreating form.

CHRISTINA (quietly) Bitch.

EIGHT

"But getting back to the tapes," said Janice. "How will it work exactly? You edit them and then publish the whole thing? Don't the people in the videos have to sign off on them first or something?"

"Of course," said Nigel. "And, obviously, we won't include anything that those involved would rather we not. But I can't imagine it being a problem," he continued. "*A Winter's Night* is an American Classic. It's like finding behind-the-scenes footage of *Gone with the Wind*."

Janice chewed the lipstick off her bottom lip before answering. "Still, it's just that while they are off camera, sometimes the actors and the crew tend to — oh, you know — let their hair down. There may be footage that might prove embarrassing. Not to me, of course," she added quickly, "but to others."

Sebastian leaned his elbows on the table

and rested his chin on his hands. With an impish grin, he said, "Me thinks the lady protests too much. Come on, darling. Let's hear it. Did you let your hair down? What did you do? Try and find out why they call him the Best Boy? You did, didn't you? Come on now, give. Tell us the whole sordid story, you saucy minx."

Janice's skin flushed. She pursed her lips together and turned her head in Sebastian's direction. "Don't be ridiculous. I did no such thing," she said stiffly. "Unlike others in this town, I have always conducted myself as a lady. I never indulged in any of that kinky hanky-panky stuff."

I wondered what kind of activity would meet the definition of both "hanky-panky" and "kinky." From the befuddled expressions of the others at the table, I suspected I was not alone. I decided it was not a question I wanted answered. Ever. "Of course you didn't, Mother," Christina said after a moment. "Bash is only teasing."

"Not that I wasn't asked to, mind you," said Janice. "I was. A lot. Oh, I could tell you some stories if I wanted to."

"What do we have to do to make sure that you don't?" Sebastian asked, his expression earnest.

"I'm only saying that there are some nasty

things that go on in this town," Janice said with an air of importance. "Some are done by the very people in this room, too."

Sebastian suddenly tensed in his chair at the sight of something behind Christina. Glancing in that direction, I saw Barry Meagher heading toward our table with a purposeful stride. "Drop it, Mother," Sebastian muttered quickly as he stood. "Barry's heading this way."

Footage from the Set of *A Winter's Tale* 5/5/96

The set is a hospital. John's character, Donny, has been injured and lies in a hospital bed. His head is bandaged and his arm is in a sling. Christina's character, Freda, is his nurse. She sits in a chair next to him. She is in a nurse's uniform. Various crew members move around them as they prepare for the next take. John idly smokes a cigarette as they wait to start. Christina flips through a magazine. Neither speaks to each other. Barry is talking to his assistant about the lighting. Off to the side, Melanie and her assistant, Sara Taylor, sit eating their lunch. Sara is about thirty years old. She is tall and thin, and her long brown hair is pulled up into a bun.

Although the camera stays focused on John, Melanie and Sara's conversation can be heard.

SARA (in a low voice) So, have you decided

what you're going to do?

MELANIE I don't know, Sara, I just don't know.

SARA But this could be your last chance! You've fought so hard for this, Melly, and now the goal is finally in sight. No one knows better than I all the crap you've had to endure for all of these years. I was there when your mom and stepdad sold you out to do that asinine show *Life with Melanie.* I've watched the men in this business try to seduce you with empty promises. I was there when the studio heads wrote you off as an insurance risk. Here's your chance to finally be able to call your own shots.

MELANIE I know, Sara. I know. It's just that I don't know if that's what I want anymore. I'm so damn tired. You have no idea how tired I am. I never knew I could feel this tired at age twenty-three. Lately, I've been wondering if it's even worth it. Let's say I finally do make it to the top. Then what?

SARA Then we make this town ours! We say which scripts you'll do and which ones you won't. *We* say who you'll work with and who can kiss your ass. We will *finally* be in charge! Think of it, Melly! We'll finally have it all.

MELANIE (voice raised) We? *We?* Who the hell do you think you are? You're my assistant, Sara. *Assistant.* Look it up if you need to be reminded of the definition. You fetch me coffee and make sure my dry cleaning is picked up. I've appreciated your work over the years, but there is no "we." There is only me. *I'm* the one who gets in front of the camera. *I'm* the one who memorizes pages and pages of dialog. *I'm* the one the paparazzi follows around morning, noon, and night. *I'm* the one who deals with the touchy feely creeps. Got it? *I* decide what I want to do with my life. And I'll decide if I want this — not you! Jesus! You're as bad as the rest of them! Everyone wants a piece of me. Everyone wants to jump on the Melanie train. Well, I'm sick of it!

John and Christina are now staring at Melanie and openly listening to her rant. Barry has stopped talking to his assistant and is also watching Melanie.

SARA That's not what I meant, Melanie. I'm sorry. I just feel protective of you. I only have your best interests at heart. You know that.

MELANIE (standing) Do I? 'Cause from

where I'm sitting, it sure sounds a hell of a lot like the same crap I've heard from everyone else over the years, "How can Melanie Summers make me more money, and what can I get her to do to get it to me faster?" You're no better than the studio heads who always try to cop a feel. The only difference is at least they're up front about it. None of them ever pretended to be my friend. But I'll give you credit for at least one thing, Sara. You helped me make up my mind. I know exactly what I'm going to do. And to hell with everyone who disagrees with me.

Melanie throws her half-eaten sandwich on the ground and storms off to her trailer. Sara sits for a second in shock and then runs after her.

SARA Melanie, wait! I'm sorry, I didn't mean it like that! Melanie! Please, listen to me!

The sound of a door slamming can be heard, followed by loud knocking.

SARA Melanie! Please let me in! Honey? I'm sorry!

The camera swings back to John and Christina. John is staring at where Melanie ran to, his cigarette seemingly forgotten in his hand. Beside him, Christina sits still reading her magazine. Her hand is shaking. Barry walks toward them.

BARRY You two ready to do the scene?
JOHN (after a quick glance at Christina) Sure. Let's do it.

Nine

Barry Meagher was an assortment of exaggerated features. Six-feet-seven and reed thin, he walked with a kind of gangly swagger. His thick silver hair was virtually untamable; no matter how short he cut it, it still managed to stick out in every direction. Coal black eyes, deep laugh lines, a crooked nose, shaggy eyebrows, and a wide mouth made up his face. Alone, each feature was unremarkable, but when combined together, it added up to that mystical x-factor which makes silk purses and wealthy used-car salesmen possible.

"Christina!" he now called out in his gravely voice. "What a night it's been! Didn't I tell you? It turned out just like I promised it would!" Christina rose from her chair, just as Barry enveloped her into an enormous hug. "I knew you were going to win the moment I saw the first rushes. You were brilliant!"

Christina hugged him back, a girlish grin on her face. "I never could have done it without you. I'm so glad you won as well!"

Barry smiled fondly down at her. It was no secret that Barry thought of Christina as the child he never had. He was both proud and protective of her, and most in the industry knew that to cross Christina was to cross Barry. "We make a good team," Barry said now. "And speaking of teams, I am really pushing Frank to cast you opposite John in *The Deposition.*"

Christina flushed and looked about to protest, when Barry lifted his hand in understanding. "I know things went to crap between you and John," he said, "mainly because John is an immature ass. But you have to admit, despite his personal failings, you two *do* work well together. And this role is an Oscar waiting to happen." He brandished his own Oscar as he added, "In the right hands, of course."

"I don't know, Barry," she began, but Janice cut her off.

"Of course, she'll take the role," Janice answered. "Just let me know what I have to do to convince Frank."

Christina closed her eyes in silent frustration. Barry's gaze slid to Janice. His lip twitched slightly. "Hello, Janice," he said.

"How are you tonight?"

Janice gave an odd laugh. "Oh, just fine. You know me. Always doing what I can to support Christina."

"Oh, I know," Barry said, as if in agreement. Something about his tone, however, suggested the opposite.

A steely expression crept into Janice's eyes. "People may think I've been pushy, but as a single parent I've had to do the work of *two* people." Pasting a smile on her face she turned to Christina and added, "Not that I minded one minute of it, of course."

Behind her, Sebastian coughed and repeated, "Of course."

Barry glanced back at Christina before saying, "No one would dare say otherwise."

Janice squared her shoulders. "I'd like to see them try." From her defiant tone, I wondered if she thought one of us was actually going to challenge her on this. Not surprisingly, no one did.

Barry gave Christina's arm a friendly squeeze, and he turned to the rest of our group. After shaking's Sebastian's hand, he focused on Mandy. Giving her a slow once over, he grinned and said, "Mandy, my dear. You look like a raspberry tart in that dress."

"I'll take that as a compliment," Mandy

replied with a wink. "After all, who can resist a raspberry tart?"

"Very few people, I imagine," Barry replied as he pulled her into a bear hug. "Certainly not me."

Mandy gave a light laugh and said, "You're incorrigible."

"Only with you," he said before his dark eyes focused on me. Releasing Mandy, he took a step toward me and said, "I never forget a pretty face. So I don't believe we've met before."

Despite the obvious line, I found myself smiling in return. Barry Meagher certainly had charm. I extended my hand and said, "I'm Nicole Martini." Tilting my head toward Nigel, I added, "This is my husband, Nigel."

Barry took my hand in his and held it while he turned to Nigel. His brows pulled up in surprise. His glance slid to Mandy and then back to Nigel. "Aren't you the couple who found the tapes?" he asked.

"That would be us," Nigel confirmed.

"Well, this is fortuitous," Barry continued, still cradling my hand in his. "I was hoping to meet you."

"As was I," Nigel said, as he held out his hand. As Barry was holding his Oscar in one hand and mine in the other, he was forced to relinquish one. It was no surprise when my hand was let go.

"What a great find. When can we expect to see them?" Barry asked as he and Nigel shook hands.

"Not for a few months yet," Nigel said, reaching for my now free hand. "We still have a lot of editing ahead of us, and I want to tape some interviews with people who were on the set. It might help to put the footage into context for the viewer."

Barry nodded in approval. "Good idea," he said. "I'd be happy to do what I can."

"We *all* will," added Janice. "I think we can all agree that it's vital that we make very sure that the final footage is an accurate portrayal of that time. We all know how easy it is to edit a story to sell a certain slant."

I was about to ask what slant she thought Nigel and I were planning to sell when a deep voice called out. "Christina! What a perfect night, eh?"

Turning, I saw the original owner of our house, Frank Samuels, walking toward us with a purposeful stride. Although he was in his early seventies, he looked far younger. Tall with broad shoulders, he moved with an athletic gait. His beard and mustache, like the hair on his head, was grey and cut short. In this sense it was at odds with his eyebrows, which were jet black and bushy. Based on his striking similarity to the woman to his right, I guessed her to be his daughter, Danielle. While she lacked both his height and facial hair, she had the same hooked nose and wide-set brown eyes of her father.

Accompanying them was John Cummings and Jules Dixon. Mandy made a soft pinging noise and in a low voice said, "Ladies and gentlemen, the Captain has turned on the 'Shit's About to Hit the Fan' light so please fasten your seatbelts and place your tray tables in their upright position. It's about to get messy."

Footage from the Set of *A Winter's Night* 5/4/96

John Cummings sits at a table off set with Christina. They are in costume and are playing gin rummy waiting for their next scene.

JOHN What time do you need to be on set tomorrow morning?

CHRISTINA (putting down a card) Eight. You?

JOHN (looking at his cards before answering) Not until ten. You want to come over?

CHRISTINA (laughing) Are you kidding? I'd love to. However, I'm not sure if I can get past Cerberus.

JOHN (puts down a card) Have you tried drugging her food?

CHRISTINA (picking up a card) Sadly, unlike Sybil and Psyche, I'm all out of spiked honeycakes.

JOHN (laughing) Well, there must be some way. Can't you tell her that you have to be here at six and come to my place?

CHRISTINA (shaking her head) No way. Ever since my kitchen scene got cut, she's been watching my every move. She's convinced that somehow I'm the reason Barry cut it.

JOHN (puts down a card) You? What the hell could you have done wrong?

CHRISTINA (shrugs and picks up a card) How much time do you have? Her theories range from my acting to my weight. But she's making damned sure that it won't happen again.

JOHN (puts down a card) And how is she going to do that?

CHRISTINA (picks up a card) The usual. Monitor everything that goes in and out of my mouth. All food and dialog must now meet with her approval.

JOHN (puts down a card) Jesus, Chris. I don't know how you put up with her.

Behind them a trailer door opens. Barry quickly emerges. He does not notice John or Christina. He walks off in a different direction, tucking in his shirt as he goes.

CHRISTINA Do you think his wife knows?

JOHN (puts down a card) Cecelia? No way. She'd kill her if she knew.

CHRISTINA (picks up a card) If I were Cecelia, I think I'd kill *him.*

JOHN (shakes his head and puts down a card) Some women are like that. They always forgive the man and blame the other woman.

CHRISTINA (pick up his card) Well, not me. I'd bash his head in. (puts down her hand) By the way, Gin.

JOHN (groaning) Ugh! You always win!

CHRISTINA (smiling) That I do.

Ten

"Well, look what the cat dragged in," Sebastian said as we watched their approach. "And by cat, I mean Jules, because she's nothing but a dirty . . ."

"Shut it, Bash," Christina snapped as she watched John and Jules's approach with a stoic expression.

Jules was your typical Hollywood starlet; a mash up of long blonde extensions, implausible breasts, a year-round tan, and blindingly white teeth. Her body was a kaleidoscope of sinuous movement. Her long hair swished, her lithe hips swayed, her round breasts shivered; all seemingly independent of one another. I watched with some admiration as her body gracefully shimmied out of the path of Seth Rogen's and James Franco's rather vigorous dance with an Oscar. Jules Dixon might not be able to act, but she sure as hell knew how to walk.

As for John, he was one of those rare actors who is just as magnetic off the silver screen as he is on it. Six-feet-four and powerfully built, he was not a man you'd overlook. His face was a composition of sharp angles and hard lines, which was saved from being too severe by the addition of a generous mouth. With a slow curl of those lips, he could convey mischief, sincerity, and sex, all with devastating effect. For John, sex appeal was a part of his DNA, no different than the color of his skin and eyes.

Christina opted to ignore them both and focused instead on Frank and Danielle. Seeing the Oscar that Danielle proudly held for her father, Christina said, "Congratulations on your win, Frank! What does this one make? Five Oscars for Best Producer?"

Frank shook his head and winked. "Six. But this one goes to Danielle," he said. "She's my good luck charm."

"She certainly is," agreed Christina before turning to Danielle. "It's lovely to see you again, Danny," she said, as she leaned in to give her a kiss on the cheek. "How have you been?"

The difference between the two women was striking, especially when you remembered that Christina, at thirty-nine, was actually four years older than Danielle. Christina was a product of Hollywood and it showed. Her skin had been pampered and polished into a perpetual dewy glow. Her lithe body was the result of years of personal trainers and strict diets. Her hair was a glossy mane of perfection.

In contrast, Danielle looked like someone you might actually know. Behind the rectangular frames of her glasses, a few laugh lines had begun to gather. Her figure, while slim, had a softness to it that spoke of the occasional lazy morning in bed rather than at the gym. Her dark hair just brushed her shoulders, cut in a manageable style that didn't require a full-time stylist.

Danielle smiled. "I've been good, thanks. Working for my dad this past year has been a dream come true."

Frank wrapped his arm around his daughter's shoulder and beamed proudly. "Danny's a real chip off the old block," he said. "She graduated with honors from Harvard just like her old man, and now she's one of our top editors."

Danielle blushed with pride. "I'm not surprised," said Christina. "I remember how much you loved film when you were younger. Speaking of which, this is the couple who found all your old tapes."

"It's nice to meet you in person," Danielle said with a shy smile. Nigel and I politely chatted with her and Frank for a few moments, while the rest of the group stood in awkward silence. Christina then turned to us and gestured to John and Jules. "This of course is John Cummings and his wife, Jules," she said. Pausing she then added, "Jules is an actress, too." This last part was said in the sing-songy voice a proud parent might use to announce successful potty-training. As if she just made a connection, Christina opened her eyes wide and said to Nigel, "Actually, you might already be familiar with Jules's work." By way of explanation, she turned to Jules and in a sweet voice explained, "Nigel's company specializes in old and lost films."

Jules's skin flushed red, and her eyes narrowed to angry slits. Next to me Mandy choked back a laugh, and then tried to cover it by pretending she was having a coughing fit. Leaning over, I patted her on the back to give the performance some credibility but I don't think we were fooling anybody. Jules appeared about to lob her own verbal attack when a loud crash caught everyone's attention.

I turned to see James Franco sheepishly grinning at a waitress. On the floor between them lay a silver platter, the remains of several Red Velvet cupcakes, most of which were on Seth Rogen and one Oscar statue.

An elegantly dressed woman standing to Franco's right shook her head as she gingerly stepped over the mess. "I swear to God, James," she said, as she moved next to Barry, "if there is so much as one dot of frosting on this dress, I'll have your ass in a sling by sunrise."

Footage from the Set of *A Winter's Night* 5/9/96

Various members of the crew are taking food from the craft table. Melanie's assistant, Sara, is among them. Her plate full, she walks past a table where John and Christina sit.

CHRISTINA (looking up) Hi, Sara. Would you care to join us?

SARA Thanks, but I've got to get Melanie her lunch first. It's been a nightmare of a day so far. I've been running around all day doing errands for Melanie, and I couldn't find this particular kind of tea she wanted, so she's going to be furious.

JOHN (laughing) As long as you're working for Mel, every day is going to be one of those days.

SARA (shooting John a stern look) You of all people should know about the stress she's under, John. I would think you'd be a little more . . . sympathetic.

JOHN (ducking his head) You're right, Sara.

I'm sorry. Well, you don't have to worry about getting her lunch. I think I saw Frank's kid bring her a tray earlier.

SARA (relieved. Takes a seat) God bless her. That's one less thing I have to deal with.

Off-camera, Barry is heard yelling for John.

JOHN Coming, Barry! Later, Chris. Later, Sara.

John shoves the final bite of his sandwich into his mouth and heads to Barry.

SARA (taking a bite of salad) Oh, my goodness! This salad is delicious! Have you had any?

CHRISTINA (her attention to where John just ran to) Yes, it's pretty good.

SARA Pretty good? It's amazing. (takes another bite) God, I think I would sell my soul for this recipe.

CHRISITINA (turning back and laughing) You'd sell your soul for lobster mac and cheese?

SARA (her face freezing in horror) What? There's lobster in this?

CHRISTINA I think so. Well, in the sauce anyway. Why? What's wrong?

Sara does not answer. She leaps to her feet and runs off.

ELEVEN

Barry smiled at the woman and said, "You do know how to make an entrance, Cecelia."

"Well, I came to get *you* to make an exit," she said. "I'm beat. I want to go home and get out of this hair shirt of a dress. Remind me never to allow myself to be talked into wearing a gown that has a built-in corset. I don't know what the hell I was thinking."

"I'll be sure to make a note of that," said Barry. "But first, I think you might be interested to meet the couple that found those tapes." Gesturing toward us, he said, "Nicole and Nigel Martini, this is my wife, Cecelia."

She blinked at us in surprise. I guessed her to be in her early fifties. Her long black hair was pulled back into a simple bun. Shrewd green eyes peered out of a face that had been allowed to tan and age. It wasn't so much beautiful as it was noteworthy.

Cocking her head to one side, she asked, "So, you're the ones who bought my brother's old house?" She threw a quick glance at Frank before continuing. "How do you like it? Is that garish statue of the well-endowed mermaid still in the backyard?"

I laughed. "Someone before us must have removed the mermaid statue," I said.

"Thank God," she said. "Damn thing was hideous."

Frank protested loudly at this. "CeCe, you're the one who gave it to me!" he argued.

She rolled her eyes. "As a joke! I never expected you to actually put the damn thing up." Leaning toward me, she added in a low voice, "My brother has a perverse sense of taste."

Barry raised his eyes to the ceiling. "*Right.* Just your brother."

Cecelia pretended to ignore him and turned to Danielle. "And how are you holding up, Danny?" she asked as she inspected her face closely. "Still having fun?"

Danielle smiled happily and snuggled in a little closer to her father's shoulder. "Oh, Aunt CeCe, I am having so much fun. I used to dream of coming to the Oscars with you all. And now that it's finally happening, I don't want it to end."

Cecelia sighed. "Well, that's youth for you. All I want to do is go home and get into bed. Speaking of which . . ." she turned questioning eyes toward Barry.

Barry nodded. "Okay. Just let me say good-bye to some people first," he said, just as Nigel's phone went off.

"Excuse me," Nigel said, pulling the phone from his coat pocket. "It's DeDee," he muttered, frowning at the readout. He shoved the phone to his ear. "Hello?" he said. His brows pulled together. "DeDee?" he asked. "What? I can barely hear you." Sticking his finger in the opposite ear, he said, "Is everything all right?" Nigel paused; his face pulled into a frown of concentration "She used to be peppy? Who used to be peppy? Sorry, DeDee but you'll have to talk louder, it's really noisy in here." He paused and closed his eyes. "Not peppy. Giuseppe? Who's Giuseppe? Wait; is he that guy down the street that keeps complaining about Skippy? Listen, I don't care *what* he says. Skippy is *not* the father. I don't care how big they are. She's not Skippy's type," Nigel's frown deepened. He bent forward in his chair in an attempt to better hear. "Slow down, DeDee. I can't understand you. *Not* Giuseppe. Okay. Sorry. Try again." Nigel's face was now squeezed shut in concentration.

"Nigel," I said, tapping him on his shoulder. "Why don't you take it outside?"

Nigel looked at me and nodded. "Hang on, DeDee. I'm moving to where it's quieter. He walked away, one finger still stuck in his left ear. "Are you saying 'used a pen'?" he shouted into the phone. "Who, Skippy? DeDee, then he's just messing with you. He only *thinks* he can write."

Nigel disappeared into the crowd still shouting into the phone. I turned back to the table, surprised to find them staring in silence back at me. "Is everything, all right?" asked Mandy. "Who's DeDee?"

I reached for my glass of champagne and took a sip. "She works for Nigel's company," I explained. "She's at our place tonight converting some of the videos we found. But it sounds like Skippy is being a nuisance."

"Oh, is Skippy your son?" Christina asked me.

I choked on my drink. "God no!" I said. "He's our *dog.* Although don't tell him that. He'd be terribly offended. As it is, I'm pretty sure he thinks Nigel and I are the pets."

Nigel returned just then and sat back

down. “Everything okay?” I asked.

Nigel shrugged and reached for his glass. “I think so. I could barely hear her. She said she’d tell us when we got home.” He took a sip of his drink.

“Is Skippy attempting to write his memoirs?” I asked.

Nigel smiled. “Something like that, I guess. DeDee kept yelling about someone named Giuseppe using a pen.”

“Do we know anyone named Giuseppe?” I asked.

Nigel shook his head. “Not as far as I know.”

“Well, in that case,” I said taking another sip. “I hope he returns our pen.”

Footage from the Set of *A Winter's Night* 5/9/96

The scene is the living room of a modest house set in 1949 Germany. Christina Franklin enters the room in character as Freda. She is wearing a simple gingham dress. Her long auburn hair falls loose around her shoulders. John Cummings, in character as Donny, stands before her wearing a suit. He holds a bouquet of flowers in his hands. Christina nods to him.

CHRISTINA/FREDA Hanna should be down in a minute. Please sit down.
JOHN/DONNY (sitting) Thank you.

Christina takes a magazine from the coffee table and begins to flip through it. John watches her.

JOHN/DONNY Aren't you going to the dance, Freda?
CHRISTINA/FREDA I am not.

JOHN/DONNY Why?

CHRISTINA/FREDA (her attention on the magazine) Because no one asked me.

JOHN/DONNY Really? I thought that you were seeing Fredrick.

CHRISTINA/FREDA (still looking at the magazine) You thought wrong.

JOHN/DONNY (frowning) Did something happen?

CHRISTINA/FREDA (angrily flipping the page) Apparently.

JOHN/DONNY Do you want to talk about it?

CHRISTINA/FREDA Do I look like I want to talk about it?

JOHN/DONNY No, I guess not. I'm sorry. I didn't mean to intrude.

CHRISTINA/FREDA (angrily throwing the magazine aside) Don't be sorry. It's not your fault.

John stares at the flowers and then looks over to the stairs as if wishing Hanna would arrive.

CHRISTINA/FREDA He's getting married.

JOHN/DONNY (startled) Who? Frederick?

CHRISTINA/FREDA (her eyes well with tears) Yes. He told me last night. He's marrying Greta Hoch.

JOHN/DONNY But, why? I thought you and he . . .

CHRISTINA/FREDA (standing) Were in love? Yes. I thought so, too. However, Greta is having his child.

JOHN/DONNY (sincerely) I'm sorry, Freda.

CHRISTINA/FREDA Don't be. Love is for fools. And I despise fools. Enjoy your dance.

Christina leaves the room. The camera swings to show the director, Barry Meagher.

BARRY Cut! Perfect! That was great, you two. Now, let's get Melanie out here and we can finish the scene.

Sara, Melanie's personal assistant, steps forward.

SARA (timidly) Um, Mr. Meagher? Melanie isn't feeling very well. And . . .

BARRY What? Again? What the hell is wrong with her THIS time? Another headache? The stomach flu? Is she as high as a kite, or is she just hung over?

SARA I promise you that she's not using, Mr. Meagher. But she was sick earlier. She couldn't seem to keep anything down. I think she may have had some of that lobster mac and cheese at lunch today. I gave her her medicine, and she's resting in her trailer now. If we could maybe give her an hour or so, I'm sure she'll feel better by then.

BARRY (glances at his watch) An hour or so? (sighing) It's four o'clock now. You know what? I'm done. I haven't been home before midnight this whole week. (yelling to crew) Okay, everyone, that's a wrap for today. Go home, go to a bar, go wherever the hell you want. I'll see you all here tomorrow at the usual ungodly hour and we'll pick up where we left off.

The actors and crew stand mutely for a moment as if unsure that Barry is serious.

BARRY Go! Before I change my mind!

Everyone departs. John grabs Christina's hand and whispers something in her ear. She smiles and nods. They quickly walk off the set. The camera swings left. It lands on Janice Franklin. She stands off to the side, watching them go. She starts to follow them, but then appears to change her mind. She walks slowly toward the trailers.

TWELVE

Seeing that Barry was about to leave, Jules moved toward him and smiled up at him from under sooty lashes. "Barry," she said sweetly, "I wanted to talk to you real quick. I've heard a rumor that you're getting ready to cast *The Deposition.* If that's true, I hope you'll give me an audition. I really think I could nail the role of the prosecutor."

Barry looked down at Jules, his expression unreadable. Cecelia was less circumspect. She regarded Jules as if she had just sprouted a second head. "Tonight is for celebrating," Barry said simply. "Not business talk."

"I know, but . . ." Jules began with a pretty pout.

Cecelia interrupted her by turning to Christina. "*You* look absolutely beautiful, Christina," she said loudly. "Life certainly seems to be agreeing with you."

Christina smiled as if she were holding

back a laugh. "It is," she said. "Of course, it's been a great night."

"The first of many, I'm sure," predicted Cecelia. Her glance skimmed over John before she added pointedly, "God knows you've earned all that and more."

Barry let out a gruff laugh. "On that note, I think we'll say our good-byes. Nicole, Nigel," he said to us, "it was nice meeting you." Taking Cecelia by the hand, he said, "Come on, my little diplomat, let's go before you start something." As he passed Christina, he kissed her cheek. "Enjoy your night, sweetheart," he said. "I'll be in touch soon."

Frank's brow wrinkled at this exchange. "Barry," he said, "before you go, I need to talk to you about something."

Cecelia let out a groan of protest. "Frank! No, I want to go home."

Frank waved away her concern. "It'll only take a few minutes, CeCe," he said.

Cecelia sighed and looked from Barry to Frank. With a resigned shake of her head, she linked her arm through Danielle's. "Come on, Danny," she said as she led her away from the table, "Let's go make ourselves comfortable at the bar. Your father's idea of a few minutes is an eternity."

The two women said their good-byes and

wandered off to the bar while Barry and Frank headed outside. "If you haven't come back in half an hour," Cecelia called over her shoulder to Barry, "I'm leaving without you!"

Barry nodded absently, his head already bent low to hear what his brother-in-law was telling him.

With their departure, the mood shifted. John and Jules now faced a table that was largely Team Christina. Sebastian regarded John with a derisive smirk. Janice pursed her lips and examined Jules as if she were something nasty on the bottom of her shoe. Mandy neatly communicated her own disapproval by simply sitting back in her chair and folding her arms across her chest. As for Christina, she stared at the bottom of her champagne glass as if it held tea leaves.

If John noticed the change in atmosphere, he didn't react. With his eyes fixed on Christina's bent head, he said, "Well, congratulations, again, Christina. Good to see Oscar will have another friend to talk to."

Christina raised her head and held his gaze. Some unspoken memory seemed to pass between them. John's mouth curved into a faint smile.

The absence of Barry and Frank made Jules bolder. She pressed her body close to

John's, her full lips curved in an over-bright smile as she regarded Christina. "Yes, congratulations, Christina," she said. "That should certainly shut up the critics who say that Hollywood ignores *older* women."

"So, how do you explain why *you're* ignored?" Sebastian asked. Jules glared at him. Sebastian leaned back in his chair and smiled. "You seem tense, Jules," he said, as he appeared to exam her face. "You're starting to get stress lines. I think you need to find something that will help you relax. What's that thing called with the needles?" he asked, turning to Christina.

"Acupuncture?" she offered.

"No, that's not it," Sebastian said with a thoughtful shake of his head. Suddenly, he snapped his fingers in remembrance. "Heroine!" he cried. "That's it. You should try heroine, Jules."

Jules flushed. "You're a bastard!" she hissed.

Sebastian shook his head as if disappointed. "Now that is tacky, Jules. Have a little decency, will you? After all, my mother is sitting right here."

What little was left of Jules's control snapped. "I've had about enough of this," she hissed at Christina. Placing her hands on the linen tablecloth, she leaned forward, shaking off John's attempts to remove her. With her mouth pinched in anger, her lips brought to mind a mutilated cherry tomato. "No," she said, her teeth clenched, "this ends now. I swear to God, Christina, if you ever pull another stunt like that pathetic speech you gave tonight, I will personally rip that rotten, black heart of yours right out of your pathetic excuse for a chest."

Several of us tried — without much success — to suppress smiles. Jules's voice had once been described as having "the breathy quality of a helium-inhaling porn star." It was perfectly suited to deliver lines of sultry seduction. Angry threats, however, came off as absurdly comical.

"You've painted me to be some home-wreaking whore, and I'm not!" she continued. "It's not my fault Johnny got sick of you and preferred someone younger, someone prettier, someone . . ."

". . . whose IQ rises to 75 on a warm summer's day?" offered Christina.

Jules's face went white under her spray tan. Angry red dots appeared on her cheeks, and her blue eyes narrowed to slits. She took a deep breath and then mouthed a vulgar, two-word suggestion to Christina.

Christina smiled sweetly up at Jules. "Sweetheart," she said, her voice sounding genuinely regretful, "how many times must we have this conversation? I've already told you — I simply can't do that until you get that rash looked at."

Jules moved to toss her drink in Christina's face, but missed and hit Janice instead. Her ensuing rant of profanity would have made even Quentin Tarantino blush. As John dragged Jules away from the table, Nigel turned to me and playfully shoved my arm. "And you worried that life after the force would be dull," he said.

I raised my glass and toasted his. "Never with you, Mr. Martini. Never with you."

Footage from the Set of *A Winter's Night* 5/4/96

Barry is sitting in his director's chair making notes on a script. A tall, good-looking man approaches. It is Frank Samuels. He is about fifty years old, has an athletic build, and is wearing a very expensive-looking tailored suit. He holds a cup of coffee in his hand.

FRANK (in a condescending voice) Hello, Barry. So, you want to tell me why Melanie called me at four this morning practically hysterical?

BARRY (at the sound of Frank's voice, Barry looks up. His expression is annoyed.) She called you? Why the hell would she call you?

FRANK I imagine because she thinks of me as someone she can trust.

BARRY Is that right? Well, how lovely for her.

FRANK So, back to my original question. Care to tell me what the hell is going on?

BARRY Gladly. Your leading lady, the ever predictable, Ms. Melanie Summers, threw a magnificent tantrum and then stormed off the set because she didn't like it when I told her that her acting had the emotional depth of a sock puppet. Her charming display of emotion — which would have been better channeled for the scene and not at me — not only set us back schedule at least a day but also put us over budget.

FRANK Dammit, Barry! You can't let things like this happen! *You* are the director. *You* are the one who is supposed to be calling the shots. *You* need to take control of your damn actors! And if *you* can't, then I'll find someone who *can*!

BARRY Are you serious? Have you completely forgotten that I never wanted Melanie Summers in the first place? *You're* the one who insisted we needed her for this film. I told you she was a mess, but you overruled me. You said she was "box office magic." Well, let me tell you something — the only magic I've seen her perform is making time, money, and my patience disappear!

FRANK Don't give me that crap! Your job as a director is to prevent the blowups! If the actors don't respect you then they'll do as they please! They're like little children, for Christ's sake! You have to treat them as such. Give them too much leeway, and they'll walk all over you. You have to take control, and show them who's boss! Do you think Scorsese got where he is by being a pushover? Do you think Coppola would let his actors run roughshod over him?

BARRY Well, last I checked, both of them have had the good sense *not* to work with Melanie Summers! I, on the other hand, wasn't given that same luxury! How about this, Frank? Since *you're* the one who insisted she be cast as the lead, how about you go and see if you can't calm the little prima donna down?

FRANK Dammit, Barry! I don't think you understand how much is riding on this movie!

BARRY On the contrary, I know exactly how much is riding on this movie — which is why I told you that casting her was a terrible idea!

FRANK Listen to me, you ungrateful bastard. I don't care if you are my brother-in-law. I stuck my neck out for you and made sure you were tapped to direct this movie. Do you really think you were the studio's first choice? They wanted Spielberg. *I* got you this movie. So, don't you dare lecture me about my casting choices, because if it weren't for me, you'd be directing the *Love Bug* movies.

BARRY (taking a deep breath) Frank, I do appreciate what you did for me. But you have to understand — the girl is a walking time bomb. She's moody, irrational, and unprofessional. You can't pin this on me — this delay sits squarely at her feet. I'm not sure if she's using again or if this is just how she is, but it's wreacking havoc with our schedule.

FRANK She's not using again. I can promise you that.

BARRY How can you be sure of that?

FRANK I just am, okay? Listen, I'll go talk to her and see if I can't calm her down. Where is she?

BARRY Last I checked she was holed up in her trailer with that poor assistant of hers. Why that woman hasn't quit or killed her is a mystery I'll never understand.

FRANK I'll see what I can do, but goddammit Barry, you have got to get control of this movie! I don't think you comprehend what I've got riding on this. If this movie fails, then I fail. And I *can't* fail! It's not an option!

BARRY You think I don't get that? You

aren't the only one whose reputation and career are on the line here. I've got just as much to lose as you do.

FRANK (scoffing) Don't flatter yourself, Barry. If I go down, it's a big event. If you go down, it'll be like the proverbial tree falling in the forest. You won't even hear about it.

Frank turns and walks away. Barry stares after him and mutters something inaudible under his breath.

Thirteen

Nigel and I soon made our excuses and left Christina's table. The rest of the night was like nothing I'd ever experienced. We were with people I was used to seeing on film, not two feet in front of me. That combined with a seemingly never-ending supply of champagne gave the evening a surreal quality. We ate cheeseburgers with Emma Stone and Jennifer Lawrence on the terrace overlooking Beverly Hills City Hall. Kevin Hart and Will Ferrell shared the last of their red velvet cupcakes with us. At one point Danielle and Cecelia came by to say their goodbyes and James Franco tried to steal Frank's Oscar from Danielle. He was outmaneuvered by Emma Stone; however, it was promptly returned. Bill Murray then recruited us to help him steal George Clooney's Oscar, only to have Mandy betray us and give it to Matt Damon. Seth MacFarlane picked us to be on his team for the

Chicken Dance Dance-Off. (The competition of which was fierce. The coveted rubber chicken was finally awarded to Sir Patrick Stewart's team, but only after a highly controversial ruling by the judges.) We sat in the photo booth and had our pictures taken, and then, at Nigel's suggestion, attempted to cram as many people as we could into it. The resulting photo looked like an indiscriminate smash up of some of Hollywood's most famous faces — plus one bare behind courtesy of the epic multitasker, James Franco. A little after three, Nigel and I decided to play *Never Have I,* which led to a mutual decision to leave just a few minutes later.

But when we pulled into our driveway, I saw that the door to our house was wide open, and I knew it was a game that we weren't going to finish.

FOURTEEN

Nigel ran in before me, yelling at me to stay in the car. Of course, I did no such thing. However, once inside the door, I stopped short in confusion. It was as if I'd suddenly stepped into one of those annoying dreams, where everything familiar is unfamiliar. The kind that you later try to describe with the unhelpful opening, "I was in our house, but it wasn't our house. You know what I mean?" Except, that this time, I did know.

All around me was utter chaos. Furniture was overturned. Emptied drawers lay in a discarded heap; their contents scattered all about. The bookshelves were bare, their volumes strewn across the floor. Atop all of it was a thick layer of feathers; the cushions they once resided in now deflated and disemboweled.

"DeDee!" Nigel and I screamed at the same time as we sprinted down the hall toward the home office. Like the front door, the office door stood wide open. Like the rest of the house, the office was in shambles. However, unlike the rest of the house, more than just material goods had been attacked. Here, the intruder had attacked the living. Bile rose in my mouth as I looked down at DeDee; her body bloodied and still.

FIFTEEN

While Nigel dialed 911, I knelt by DeDee's prone form. Gently pressing two fingers to her neck, I closed my eyes, silently praying that she was alive. A few heart-wrenching seconds later, I felt a pulse. It was faint and thready, but it was there. I glanced up at Nigel. "She's alive, but barely," I said. "We need to get her to a hospital now."

Nigel nodded and quickly relayed all the necessary information to the operator. I remained on the floor next to DeDee. Blood caked her hair and face. Her right eye had started to swell, the delicate skin around it already turning an ugly shade of purple. Gingerly, I placed her right hand in mine and leaned close to her ear.

"DeDee? Can you hear me," I asked, trying to keep my voice calm and sure. "Nigel and I are here, and we've called for help. An ambulance is on its way. You're going to be fine, DeDee. Do you understand? You are going to be fine. I just need you to hang on until the paramedics get here. Can you do that for me? You need to be strong, DeDee. I know you can do it. Hang on. Help is almost here." Her hand remained limp and unmoving.

Nigel hung up the phone and knelt down beside me. "Jesus," he whispered, as he looked at DeDee, "who would have done this?"

"I have no idea," I said, "but whoever it was wanted her dead."

"Who would want to hurt DeDee?" he asked. "Do you think her ex might have followed her out here?"

"He might have, but for what purpose? Why would he come after her now after all this time? And why would he ransack our house if he just wanted to hurt DeDee?"

"I don't know, Nic, but whoever did this was an animal. Animals aren't always known for their rational thought."

At the word "animal" we both stared at each other, eyes wide. "Where's Skippy?" I said, just as Nigel leapt to his feet.

"Skippy?!" he yelled as he ran from the room. "Skippy!"

I sat frozen to the floor, DeDee's inert hand in mine. As I listened to Nigel's increasingly panicked voice call out for

Skippy, an icy numbness spread through my heart. I had worked some gut-wrenching cases when I was in New York, but the worst ones were those involving kids. To have to look into the anguished eyes of a frantic parent and tell them that their worst nightmare had come true was its own kind of hell. As I listened to the sounds of Nigel tearing from room to room in search of Skippy, I had a greater empathy for those parents' pain. Skippy wasn't our child, but he was a part of our family. The idea that he might be hurt — or even worse — made me physically ill. Not being able to help look for him myself only increased my distress. After what seemed like an eternity, but was probably only two or three minutes, I heard Nigel cry out in relief, "Skippy! Oh, thank God! Are you all right, boy? It's okay, it's okay. I missed you, too. Skippy, don't jump on me! Skippy, easy boy!" The next sound was that of Nigel falling to the floor underneath an apparently enthusiastic and unharmed Skippy. Seconds later, I heard the piercing wail of the ambulance's siren as it sped toward our house.

I sagged against the side of the desk, not sure which sound gave me more relief.

Sixteen

I let the paramedics in and rushed them to where DeDee was. After answering what few questions I could, I stepped back and let them do their job. I only interrupted them once, asking, "Is she going to be okay?"

One of the paramedics, a burly blonde with a tattoo peeking out from under his white sleeve, glanced over his shoulder at me. "Hard to say," he said, not unkindly. "She's in pretty bad shape. It's lucky that you found her when you did. A little while longer, and I don't think there'd be much hope. But she's in good hands now. We'll do what we can."

I nodded and walked out into the hallway, just as Nigel brought Skippy downstairs. Seeing me, Skippy repeated the ebullient greeting he had given Nigel. His paws draped over my shoulders, he whined and licked my face with an enthusiasm I didn't try to temper. "Where was he?" I asked

Nigel as I happily pressed my face against the dense fur on Skippy's neck.

"DeDee must have put him up in our bedroom," he answered. "Speaking of which, I suggest you stay out of there if you want to keep your current benevolent mind-set about Himself."

I glanced up at Nigel. "Why? What did he do?"

Nigel sighed and scratched Skippy behind his ear. "Well, do you remember our curtains?"

"Yes."

"Good. Because that's the only place they exits now; in our memories. Same thing goes for the carpet in front of the door. Oh, and while we're on the subject, the door," Nigel added with a shake of his head.

I ran my hands over Skippy to make sure he wasn't hurt. As I did, he covered my face with slobbery kisses and whined as if to apologize. "Poor baby," I said. "It's okay, Skippy. You were trying to get out to help DeDee, weren't you?" I asked.

Skippy gave a short bark, his soft brown eyes staring intently into mine. There are times when I think Skippy is more intelligent than the majority of our population. And then there are times like now, when I know he is.

The paramedics rolled DeDee out on a gurney. She lay still and unconscious. What little of her face I could see from beneath the gauze bandages looked suddenly smaller and older. I gently pushed Skippy off of me and asked, "Which hospital are your taking her to?"

"Cedars-Sinai," said the blonde paramedic rapidly as he continued to monitor her vital signs. "Once you're finished with the police, you can see her there."

I nodded, my throat tightening at the sight of DeDee's battered face. Now that the paramedics had her, all of my earlier adrenaline vanished. Exhaustion now seeped through my body. Tears pricked the back of my eyes. Nigel wrapped his arm around my shoulder. "She's going to be fine," he murmured softly as he pressed his face into my hair. "DeDee's a fighter." I turned into his chest as he pulled me into his arms and hoped to hell he was right.

Seventeen

No sooner had the paramedics rushed DeDee outside to the ambulance than two police officers stepped into the foyer. The first was a small, wiry woman I guessed to be about thirty-five. Her clear grey eyes regarded me as if I were a specimen under glass. The second officer was tall with broad-shoulders. His dark hair was shaved close to his skull. Neither seemed particularly happy to be here. I was not unsympathetic.

"You the ones that found the victim?" the first officer asked, her voice clipped.

"DeDee. Yes, we found her," Nigel answered, still holding me tight against his chest.

"I see," she said, flipping open a notebook. "And her full name?"

"Dorothy Deanne Evans," Nigel said. "She's our employee. She was house-sitting for us tonight."

"I see," she said. "And you are . . . ?"

"I'm Nigel Martini and this is my wife, Nicole."

"I'm Officer Hax and this is Officer Kelly," she said jerking her chin toward her partner. Officer Kelly nodded. Nigel and I nodded back.

"I was just about to make some coffee," I said, reluctantly stepping out of Nigel's embrace. "Is it okay if we continue this conversation in the kitchen?"

"That's fine," Officer Hax said. Officer Kelly nodded. Apparently, he wasn't much of a talker. Not that I cared. It was almost four-thirty in the morning. I wasn't really in the mood for a lot of chitchat either.

I led them down the hallway. While I busied myself scooping beans into the coffee maker, Nigel and the officers seated themselves at our kitchen table. Skippy sprawled on his back at Nigel's feet, demanding a belly rub. Nigel obliged.

"So, why don't you tell me what happened?" Officer Hax began as she flipped to a new page of her notebook.

"We got home around three-thirty and saw that the front door was open. We found the place the way it is now — trashed. Nic and I called out for DeDee, but she didn't answer. We found her in the study beat up and unconscious, and called 911," Nigel said.

"Did Ms. Evans have any enemies you know of?" Officer Hax asked.

Nigel shook his head. "Not that I know of," he answered, as he shrugged out of his tuxedo jacket. "I mean, I don't think she's on very good terms with her ex-husband, but they've been divorced for several years now, and as far as I know, he's never tried to contact her."

Officer Hax scribbled in her notebook. "Do you know the ex's name and address?" she asked.

"Reggie Evans," said Nigel. "I don't know his exact address. He lives in Tallahassee, Florida. He runs a plumbing business there. Or at least he used to."

"I see," replied Officer Hax as she jotted this down. "And do you know why they divorced? Was it friendly? Acrimonious?"

"I'd say it was pretty acrimonious," I answered as I pulled out cups, cream, and sugar and loaded everything onto a coffee tray.

"Oh? Why was that?" Officer Hax asked turning to me.

"Apparently, Reggie wasn't a big fan of the Seventh Commandment," I said.

Officer Hax's eyebrows pulled together.

"Right. Wait. The Seventh. Is that Don't Kill or Don't Commit Adultery?"

"Adultery," I said as I carried the coffee tray to the table.

"Reggie liked to stick his plunger where it didn't belong," Nigel explained. We all stared at him. Nigel blinked and then looked at me. "What?" he asked.

"Have some coffee, Nigel," I said, handing him a cup. He took a large sip and closed his eyes. "You'll have to excuse us," I said to the officers. "It's been a long day. How do you take your coffee, Officer Hax?"

"With cream. No sugar," replied Officer Hax. "Thanks."

After I handed her a cup, I turned to Officer Kelly. "Coffee?" I offered, holding up the pot.

He nodded. "Black. Thanks," he said, before falling silent again. Once I'd poured out the coffee, I sat down next to Nigel.

"So, we were talking about the ex-husband," Officer Hax prompted.

"Yes. Well, DeDee was understandably upset when she discovered Reggie's extracurricular activities," I explained. "Especially as he was mixing business with pleasure, so to speak. DeDee had worked hard to help Reggie grow that business, so she was understandably angry."

Officer Hax nodded. "Okay," she said, adding more to her notebook. "But I feel like there's a 'which is why' part coming up pretty soon," she said, glancing back up at me.

I took a sip of my coffee. "There is. When DeDee found out what Reggie was up to, she went to his office and . . . well, she smashed up his equipment. I could see how Reggie might still be upset about that."

"What was the extent of the damage?" asked Officer Hax as she reached for her coffee cup.

"Oh, nothing permanent," I assured her. "But Reggie was in the hospital for a week or so, and I believe he had to sit on a pillow for a month after that."

Officer Hax froze, her coffee cup poised mid-air. "I thought you were referring to his plumbing business equipment," she said, putting her cup down and picking up her notebook.

"Oh, DeDee smashed that up as well," said Nigel.

Officer Hax stared at Nigel a beat and then jotted something into her notebook. "Okay, I'd say we definitely need to get in touch with Mr. Evans. Now, what time did Ms. Evans arrive at your house last night?"

"Probably around five o'clock or so," I

answered. "She met us at the Dolby Theater and brought Skippy back to our house."

Officer Hax took a sip of her coffee. "I gather then that you two were at the Oscars last night?"

"Yes. And then the Vanity Fair party afterward," I answered.

"Right. Okay. You said Ms. Evans is your employee. What is it that she does?" Officer Hax asked.

"She works on film restoration," Nigel answered. "Our company restores old and damaged films. DeDee was working on transferring old videos that were taken on the set of *A Winter's Night* tonight."

Officer Hax's head popped up, her professional façade gone. "Seriously?" she asked, her eyes bright. "You two are the ones who found those tapes?"

"That's us," I said.

"I was just reading about those," she said. "Is it true that Melanie Summers is on them?"

I told her that it was.

"Wow. I loved her movies," said Officer Hax. "Every Christmas, my mom and I would watch *A Miraculous Moment.* She was such a good actress."

"She was," Nigel agreed.

"I've got to tell you, I'm really looking

forward to seeing them," said Officer Hax.

"You and everyone else . . ." Nigel stopped and looked at me, but I was already out of my seat and running down the hall toward the office.

Eighteen

"They're gone!" I groaned, after checking the computer's disk drive. "Nigel, the tapes are gone!"

Nigel skidded into the room two seconds after me. Normally he would have beaten me — at six four, Nigel's legs are much longer than mine — but Skippy had joined in the race. Two people barreling down a narrow hallway is one thing; add in a hundred-and-thirty-pound bullmastiff with questionable depth perception, and it becomes a mini Pamplona.

Despite my announcement, Nigel checked the computer for himself. I didn't take it personally. He pressed already lit elevator buttons, too. "Damn it," he muttered as he smacked the hard drive in frustration.

"Would these missing tapes be the ones from *A Winter's Night*?" Officer Hax asked.

Nigel flung himself in the desk chair and began frantically clicking open all the computer files. "Damn it, damn it, damn all to hell!" he now yelled.

"How much is gone?" I asked.

"I don't know for sure. But I'd say three, maybe four tapes. And yes, Officer Hax, we're talking about the tapes from *A Winter's Night.* DeDee said she was going to work on a few of them while she was here," Nigel said as he rubbed his hands over his face in frustration. I moved next to him and put my hand on his shoulder. He put his hand over mine, but he didn't say anything.

"Did anyone know that Ms. Evans was here and working on the tapes?" Officer Hax asked.

Nigel shook his head and started to reply, when I cut him off. "Nigel," I said. "The phone call."

Nigel jerked his head back, his startled eyes meeting mine. "Shit," he said.

"Yeah," I said. "Shit."

"So, I'm guessing that that's a 'yes' as well," said Officer Hax, flipping open another page of her notebook. "Do me a favor, Kelly. Go get me my cup of coffee. I have a feeling that we're going to be here a little while longer."

Nineteen

"Tell me about this phone call," Officer Hax prompted.

"It was from DeDee," Nigel said. "I guess it was around eleven when she called. We were still at the Vanity Fair event, and it was really loud. I could barely hear her. At first I thought she was calling about Skippy. Well, I should back up. I thought she said she was calling about Giuseppe."

"And who is Giuseppe?" Officer Hax asked.

Nigel shrugged. "I have no idea. I thought it might be a neighbor of ours from down the street. His Labrador recently had puppies, and he's convinced that Skippy here is the father." He looked down at Skippy, who still lay sprawled on his back, his paws in the air and his tongue hanging to one side of his mouth. "It's ridiculous, of course. Skippy barely knows her."

Office Hax stared in silence at Nigel for a

beat. Then she scribbled something into her notebook. I could only imagine what.

"But it turns out she wasn't talking about our neighbor," Nigel continued. "And in any case, his name is Gaspari, not Guiseppe."

"I see," said Officer Hax. "Who was she talking about then?"

Nigel shook his head. "That's the thing. I honestly don't know. It sounded like she was saying something about this Giuseppe having our pen, but as I said it was impossible to hear in there. I went to take the call outside, but DeDee said she'd just tell me when we got home."

Officer Hax rubbed a tired hand over her face. "So, perhaps she was scared about this Giuseppe person?"

"No," said Nigel leveling her with a dark look. "While I couldn't hear her exact words, DeDee definitely wasn't scared. I wouldn't have stayed at that party if I thought DeDee was in any kind of danger or was even the slightest bit nervous."

I put my hand over Nigel's. "Nigel considers his staff as an extension of his family, Officer Hax. I don't think DeDee thought she was in any danger when she called us."

Officer Hax nodded. "I'm only asking questions, Mr. Martini. I'm not accusing you or passing judgment. I just want to get an idea as to her state of mind when she called."

"I understand," said Nigel. "She seemed fine."

"Can you remember who might have overheard your phone call?" she asked next.

I recited the names of those who were at the table at the time. Officer Hax dutifully wrote it all down. "Of course, I walked away to try and hear her better," Nigel added. "Anyone around me could have overheard what I was saying."

"I understand. Still, this is a start. Is there anything else you can think of?" Officer Hax continued. "Anyone else you know that might have wanted to get those tapes?"

Nigel and I looked at each other and simultaneously said, "Mr. Luiz."

Officer Hax flipped open a new page of her notebook. "Okay. Who is Mr. Luiz?" she asked.

I quickly explained about the reporter who approached us on the red carpet. "Do you still have his card?" she asked.

Nigel fished it out of his pocket and handed it to her. She stared down at the card. "David Luiz," she read. "Hollywood Foreign Press Association. Brazil."

"Isn't there a famous Brazilian soccer

player named David Luiz?" Officer Kelly suddenly asked.

Officer Hax turned and stared at him. "There is. What's your point?" she asked.

Officer Kelly shrugged. "Just wondering if there is a connection."

Officer Hax stared at him for a beat and finally said, "I don't see how there could be, but if you want to check into it, by all means, go ahead."

Officer Hax then shut her notebook and stood up. "Thank you for your time," she said. "Hopefully, Ms. Evans will recover sufficiently to be able to answer more questions for us. In the meantime, I suggest you two get some sleep. We'll be in touch."

Officer Kelly stood as well. He looked at both of us and then cleared his throat. "Don't worry. We'll get the person that did this. My dad always said, it's always darkest before the dawn. Thanks for the coffee," he added as he put down his cup and followed Officer Hax out of the room.

Nigel and I sat together in silence. At the sound of the front door closing, Nigel turned to me with tired eyes. "Isn't it darkest in the middle of the night?" he asked.

"That's always been my understanding."

He looked back toward the door. "I think

I like Officer Kelly better when he doesn't talk," he said.

Twenty

Nigel and I changed out of our formal attire and took a quick shower before driving to Cedars-Sinai. There we met with DeDee's attending physician, Dr. Leah Boht. She was a petite woman with high cheekbones and skin the color of warm caramel. Dr. Boht told us that DeDee had suffered several broken bones in her face, a broken shoulder, and three broken ribs. "She's a tough lady," Dr. Boht said. "And damned lucky, too. As bad as it is, it could have been much worse. It's a good thing that you found her when you did. You saved her life."

"Is she awake? Can we see her?" I asked.

"I don't see why not," said Dr. Boht. "As long as you keep the visit short. However, she may be sleeping. We gave her something for her pain."

She motioned for us to follow her down the hall to DeDee's room. "Did she say anything to you?" I asked. "Anything about who did this to her?"

Dr. Boht shook her head. "No, I'm sorry. She hasn't said anything yet." She stopped in front of a doorway and motioned for us to go in. "Keep it brief," she reminded us.

Nigel and I walked into the room. DeDee lay on the bed, her eyes closed. Bandages covered the rest of her face. "Hey DeDee," I said softly. At the sound of my voice, her eyelids fluttered and opened. Nigel and I smiled at her.

"Hey there," Nigel said. "How are you doing?"

DeDee's eyes flickered from Nigel to me and then back to Nigel. "Not so good," she croaked.

"Well, the doctor tells us that you're going to be just fine," I said, taking a step closer to the bed.

"That's good to know," she said.

"Do you know who did this to you?" I asked.

DeDee started to shake her head, but the movement caused too much pain. "Where am I?" she asked, her voice groggy.

"Cedars-Sinai Hospital," I answered as I gently reached for her hand.

"Oh," she said. After a brief pause, she looked at my hand and then at me, her eyes questioning.

"What is it?" I asked.

DeDee held my gaze. "Well, for starters," she said, "who are you?"

Twenty-One

Back in the hallway, I stared at Dr. Boht. "Amnesia?" I repeated dumbly.

Dr. Boht nodded. "I'm afraid so," she said. "It's not uncommon, especially with these kinds of head injuries. In most cases, however, it's temporary. Does she have any family that you know of?"

I nodded. "Yes. She has a sister in New Jersey. I'll call her."

Dr. Baht nodded. "Fine. If she has any questions, have her call me. It might be helpful for her to come out, if she can. Familiar faces can help jog the memory back."

I nodded again, my movements wooden. "Right. I'll see if I can book her a flight."

Dr. Boht reached over and touched my arm. "She'll be fine. I promise you. It just takes time," she said kindly. "Now, I think the best thing you two can do is to go home and get some sleep," she said. "You look exhausted. If there is any change in Ms. Evans's condition, we'll call you right away."

Nigel and I thanked Dr. Boht and numbly walked out of the hospital and to the parking garage. I then called DeDee's sister, Nancy, and relayed what little information I had. After arranging a flight and hotel for her, Nigel and I drove home. There we collapsed into bed, where we remained for several hours. When I finally awoke, it was to the sensation of a long body stretched lazily over mine. Opening my eyes, I found myself looking up into two brown ones.

"Nigel?" I said, as a nose nuzzled against my neck.

"Hmmm?"

"Are you comfortable?" I asked.

"Very. Why?"

"Because, I'm not. Help me out, will you?"

Next to me, Nigel rolled over, laughing when he saw me pinned underneath Skippy's massive frame. "Aw, don't make him get off of you," he said. "He's just saying 'hi.' Besides, he looks so comfy."

"That's great, but I think my lungs are in danger of collapsing." Skippy wagged his tail and began to enthusiastically lick my face. "That is, if I don't drown first," I amended, as I tried to push Skippy off of me. With Nigel's help, I was finally able to squeeze out from under him, and roll toward Nigel's side of the bed. Skippy happily settled into my vacated spot and laid his massive head on my pillow.

"See, he just wanted to snuggle with us," Nigel said as he used his T-shirt to wipe the drool off of my face.

"That's not snuggling," I said. "That's full-body-contact sleeping. In fact, in some countries I think we'd be legally engaged now. I feel like I'm covered from head to toe in dog slobber," Nigel laughed and continued to wipe off Skippy's drool, until I pointed out that "head to toe" was only an expression, and that I wasn't comfortable performing in front of an audience. Nigel conceded the point and made the necessary adjustments. When we finally stumbled out of our bedroom sometime later, Skippy was patiently waiting for us on the living room couch.

While Nigel made us coffee, I attempted to shove Skippy off the couch. After awhile, I gave up. When Nigel returned, I was curled up in the club chair reading the recaps of the evening. There were pictures of various celebrities as they left the Vanity Fair Party: Frank and Barry clinking their Oscars together in celebration; an unsmiling Jules and John as they ducked into a black limo; and one that seemed to catch a laughing Christina, Sebastian, James Franco, and Seth Rogen as they ran from something inside. There was also a shot of Nigel and me. Nigel's face wore an easy smile. Mine looked like I'd just been goosed. Which was only fair, seeing as I had been.

"You made the gossip page," I said as he handed me my coffee.

Nigel took a deep breath. "I was afraid of that," he said as he took a seat in the chair opposite mine. "Let me just start by saying that it was David's idea to begin with. You see, he bet me . . ."

"Nigel, it's an article about the Oscars," I said before taking a sip of my coffee.

Nigel affected a look of relief. "Oh. That does make more sense, now that I think about it."

I smiled at him over the rim of my cup. "But since you mentioned it, what bet?"

"Exactly," said Nigel with a wink. "Best to play it dumb should anyone ask."

I rolled my eyes and resumed reading the paper. After a minute, I said, "Why do they always have to mention the fact that I'm an ex-detective like I did a stint in prison?"

Nigel laughed. "What did they say this time?"

"Among last night's attendees was Movie

Magic founder, Nigel Martini," I quoted. *"The former playboy attended the ceremony with his wife, Nic, and their dog, Skippy. Mr. Martini looked impeccable as always in a tux by Oscar de la Renta while Mrs. Martini donned a lavender gown by Christian Dior — a far cry from her days in uniform as a New York City Homicide Detective. Not to be outdone, Skippy was also dressed for the occasion, sporting a black silk bowtie on his stately neck."*

I threw the paper down. " 'A far cry from her days in uniform'? Honestly? Detectives don't even wear uniforms."

"A fact which, as I've said before, makes role-playing all the more difficult. But look on the bright side. You got top billing over Skippy."

After we finished our coffee, we inspected the damage from DeDee's attacker. "This makes no sense to me," he said as we surveyed the living room. "If it were the tapes that they were after, why would they rip open our cushions? They can't have possibly thought that we would have hidden them in there, could they?"

The room was certainly a disaster. It looked as if someone had turned the room upside down, shaken it violently, and once it was righted again, ripped open everything that hadn't fallen open. "Is anything missing?" I asked.

"Besides the tapes — no," he answered. "Thank God, the rest of the tapes are at the office. At least they didn't get all of the footage."

I drank from my cup. "I'm guessing that the person who did this wanted to draw attention away from the tapes," I said. "I mean, even we didn't think of it right away."

Nigel walked over to the desk and bent down to put the drawers back in, while I began to put books back on their shelves. "If that's the case, then someone went to a hell of a lot of trouble," he groused.

"That they did," I agreed. "But, I'll be damned if I let it pay off for them."

Twenty-Two

Nigel and I spent the rest of the day undertaking the Sisyphean task of trying to put the house back into some semblance of order. By nine-thirty, I was tired, grumpy, and seriously considering leveling the house with a boulder just to complete the theme. I flopped heavily onto the couch, unleashing a cloud of feathers from the rent cushions in the process. The feathers swirled around me, sticking to my hair and clothes. "I think it might just be easier to move," I groused as I watched Skippy bark and pounce on those that floated to the ground.

Nigel plucked a feather from my hair. "You need dinner," he said. "You always get cranky when you have an empty stomach. Just sit here and relax while I go get us something." He removed a few more feathers from my person before kissing the top of my head and disappearing into the kitchen. I closed my eyes rather than look at the mess around me. I must have dozed off because it seemed that only a few moments later Nigel had returned. "Here we are," he said. "Dinner is served."

Opening my eyes, I looked at the tray on the coffee table in front of me and blinked in confusion. "We're having a bottle of Merlot for dinner?"

Nigel nodded as he uncorked the bottle. "It's an old family recipe," he said. "But, to be safe, I also ordered some Chinese food from that place you like."

"You're always thinking, Mr. Martini," I said as I carefully made room for Nigel on the couch so as not to upset any more feathers. I needn't have bothered. With a deftly executed backward hop, he vaulted onto the couch. A flurry of white plumes exploded around us. Skippy immediately jumped back to attention, alternately barking and trying to catch each and every feather.

"Forgive me for asking this," I said, as I pulled a feather out of my mouth, "but why?"

Nigel brushed a feather from his face. "You never wanted to see what it would be like inside a snow globe?" he asked as he leaned forward to pour me a glass of wine.

"No," I said, "not after the age of six anyway. However, I'm guessing you did."

He nodded and handed me my glass of wine. "I have to admit. It's not as fun as I expected."

I tipped my head in acknowledgement. "Few things are."

Nigel wrapped his arm around my shoulder and pulled me close. "Oh, I wouldn't say *that,* Mrs. Martini."

By the time the food arrived, Nigel and I had moved to the floor, and my mood had vastly improved. The feathers had settled; with the majority of them lodged in Skippy's fur. Lying on his back with his paws in the air, he now resembled a molting yeti. Nigel spread a blanket on the floor in front of the couch, and we ate our dinner picnic-style from the white take-out boxes.

"What do you think could be on those tapes that somebody was willing to almost kill DeDee?" Nigel asked as he speared a shrimp with lobster sauce and popped it into his mouth.

"No idea," I said as I chewed on a steamed dumpling. "From what I've seen of the footage so far, things seem pretty standard: petty fights, jealousies, ruthless ambition, and inflated egos."

"None of which are exactly unheard of in this town," he said.

"None of which are exactly unheard of in

any town," I corrected, as I stuck my chopstick in another dumpling and shoved it in my mouth.

"Janice seemed to hint that there were some untoward behavior on the set," Nigel said.

"Janice strikes me as someone who seeks out untoward behavior," I said, while chewing.

"Careful, darling. You know the affect a cynical woman with a mouth full of food has on me."

"I do indeed," I answered. "It's one of the main reasons you married *me.*"

"Well, that and you owned a gun at the time."

"I still own the gun," I pointed out.

"Which is why we're *still* married," Nigel answered.

I finished the steamed dumplings and a few mouthfuls of the fried rice and leaned back against the couch. "I suppose we should clean up and start watching the remaining tapes," I said with a yawn.

"I suppose we should," Nigel agreed.

We both fell asleep sitting there. When I awoke the next morning, I saw that Skippy had kindly helped us clean up by eating the rest of the take-out.

Footage from the Set of *A Winter's Night* 5/7/96

The set is a nightclub. Melanie and John are in character as Hanna and Donny. Melanie sits alone at a table. She is wearing a red cocktail dress with a heart-shaped neckline and capped sleeves. Her hair is styled in a top reverse roll. John stands next to her. He is wearing a dark suit. His right eye is blackened and there is a butterfly bandage over his eyebrow. In his hand is a lit cigarette.

JOHN/DONNY You look lovely tonight, Hanna. But then, you always look lovely.

MELANIE/HANNA (looking down at her drink) Donny, don't.

JOHN/DONNY Don't what? Tell the girl I love that she's beautiful?

MELANIE/HANNA You know what will happen if my father finds out you were talking to me. I won't let you get hurt again.

JOHN/DONNY (takes a drag off of his cigarette and then puts it out on the

table's ashtray) What can he do that he hasn't already done? Having me beat up is nothing compared to having my heart broken. Dance with me, Hanna. Please. Please just let me hold you one more time.

MELANIE/HANNA(looks up) Oh, Donny. I . . . I . . . (no longer in character) Oh, Christ, I think I'm going to be sick!

BARRY CUT!

Melanie stumbles out of her chair and into a surprised Johnny. She loses her balance and lands on her knees at Johnny's feet. She begins to retch.

JOHN (horrified) Jesus! Are you kidding me? What the hell is wrong with you?

MELANIE What does it look like? I'm sick, you jackass!

JOHN You threw up on my shoes!

MELANIE Yeah. I kind of noticed that *especially as I'm the one down here puking!*

Sara Taylor, Melanie's personal assistant, rushes forward. Her face is worried.

SARA Melanie! Oh, dear God. Are you okay? What happened?

MELANIE Hello, Sara. I'm not okay. Although I can certainly see why you might be confused, as I normally enjoy vomiting all over myself and in front of an audience.

Sara gently helps Melanie to her feet.

SARA I'm sorry. Here, let me help you get cleaned up.

BARRY (angrily) What the hell is going on, Melanie? Are you using again? I swear to God, if you are, you are out! Do you hear me! OUT! I can't deal with your crazy drama anymore!

MELANIE Shut up, Barry. I'm not using. I just don't feel well. As you can see for yourself. (Melanie pushes Sara away) I don't need your help, Sara. Thank you. I can manage. And you can stop glaring at me, John. It's not like I puked on you on purpose. Although, I must admit, it was somewhat cathartic.

JOHN I can honestly say, I don't really care what your purpose was in as much as the result is the same. I am covered in vomit. Speaking of which, can someone get me a goddamn towel?

Melanie walks away to her trailer. Barry turns to Sara.

BARRY What the hell is going on, Sara? Is she using again?

SARA (shaking her head) No, sir. Not at all. It's probably an allergic reaction. You know how she's allergic to shellfish. I think there was salmon on the craft table this morning for breakfast.

BARRY (nodding calmly) Yes, well that would explain it . . . (now yelling) *if salmon were a shellfish*!

SARA (blushing) I'm sorry, Mr. Meagher. Of course, it isn't. But Ms. Summers isn't using. I promise you. She just doesn't feel well. She says she's been under a lot of stress lately. You know how artists are. They get emotional. They feel things differently from the rest of us. It can be hard to understand them sometimes, but I guess that's what sets them apart from the rest of us.

BARRY, (sighing) Just because you don't understand her, Sara, doesn't mean she's an artist. Most likely it means she's impossible to understand.

Twenty-Three

When we got to the hospital the next morning, DeDee was asleep. Her sister, Nancy, was by her side. Like DeDee, Nancy had a prominent nose, wiry build, and a penchant for cutting to the chase.

"Did the police find the bastard that did this yet?" Nancy asked us without preamble.

"Not yet," I answered.

Nancy turned back to look at DeDee's bruised face. "Well, I'm definitely going to want a few minutes alone with the son of a bitch when they do," she said.

"You and about ten other people," Nigel told her, "but I'll make sure you're at the front of the line."

"Has there been any change in her condition?" I asked.

Nancy shook her head. "Not really. She said I look familiar, which is a good sign, but the rest is still a blank."

We sat with Nancy until DeDee woke up.

Unfortunately, she still had no idea who Nigel and I were, and our presence only seemed to agitate her. With Nancy promising to keep us informed, we left and returned home. There we found two police cars waiting for us in our driveway.

In the first, were Officers Hax and Kelly. In the second, was a new face. It was a handsome face, too; dark blonde hair, steely blue eyes, and a jaw that appeared to have been chiseled out of granite. The face was attached to a man I guessed to be in his mid-forties. Unlike Hax and Kelly, he was not wearing a uniform. Instead, he wore a tailored blue blazer, a white linen shirt, fitted dark jeans, and a self-satisfied smirk. From the way Hax and Kelly deferred to him, I gathered he was their superior. Back in New York, a guy in a cop car who looked like this was more likely to be the criminal than the officer. I mentally shook my head. Every time I thought I had adjusted to California, something like this happened, and I realized that I'd probably never get used to it.

"Hello, Officer Hax, Officer Kelly," Nigel said, as he got out from the driver's side. Looking at the new guy, Nigel put out his hand, "I don't believe we've met. I'm Nigel Martini. And you are?"

"Detective Jack Brady," he answered, shaking Nigel's hand. Detective Brady was a few inches shorter than Nigel and a little broader in the shoulders, but other than that, they shared the same lean athletic build. "This is my wife, Nicole," Nigel now said, turning to me.

"Hello, Detective Brady," I said, as I held out my hand as well. "What can we do for you?"

Detective Brady shook my hand firmly, but did not immediately answer my question. He stared at me a beat as if faintly amused. Releasing my hand, he said, "I know that you spoke with Officer Hax and Kelly earlier, but I just wanted to follow up and make sure that Hax covered everything she was supposed to. You know, crossing the "T's" and dotting the "I's."

I stole a glance at Officer Hax. Her expression was blank. She'd make a hell of a poker player. "Officer Hax seemed very thorough," I said. "Was there anything in particular you wanted to clarify?"

Detective Brady gave an almost apologetic shrug. "Nothing in particular. But, Hax here tells me that you used to work for the New York City Police Department. Mrs. Martini, is that correct?"

"For six years," I answered with an affirming nod.

Detective Brady's smile dimmed. "You were an officer?" he asked, his tone doubtful.

"Oh, no," I said with a shake of my head. His smile reappeared. "I was a detective," I clarified. "I worked homicide."

The smile now completely vanished. A faint line formed between his eyebrows. With a shake of his head, he turned back to Officer Hax, saying, "Guess you were right, Hax. Looks like I owe you a beer." Officer Hax breathed heavily out of her nose, but didn't respond. Detective Brady turned back to me.

I raised a questioning eyebrow. Detective Brady saw it and let out a small laugh. "Sorry," he said with a shrug, "It's just that you don't look like any detective *I've* ever met. Of course, I mean that as a compliment."

"I'm sure you do," I said.

Officer Hax coughed into her hand. Detective Brady glanced at her and then looked back to me. "So why did you leave?" he asked. He jerked his chin toward Nigel. "Decide to finally settle down and get married?"

"Not at all," I answered. "I was told that there were going to be some . . . oh, let's just say, 'openings' in the Beverly Hills Department and was asked to consider throwing my hat in the ring."

The line reappeared between Detective Brady's eyebrows. "Openings?" he repeated.

I nodded and leaned forward. "Something about 'spring cleaning' and 'outdated gender attitudes,' " I said in a low voice, "but I probably shouldn't say any more until it's official." Detective Brady blinked at me and rocked back on his heals. "Was there anything else you wanted to talk to us about, Detective?" I asked. "Is there any news on who might have attacked our employee?"

Detective Brady cleared his throat before answering. "Well, that's not something I think we should discuss in your driveway. Would it be possible to go inside for a moment so we can talk?"

"Of course," I said. Nigel and I led the three officers up the slate walkway and inside the house. Skippy met us with a tennis ball in his mouth. Detective Brady stared at Skippy in surprise. "Wow. You don't see too many Great Danes around," he said.

"That's true," I agreed. "Especially in this house," I added, as I took a seat on the couch next to Nigel. Meeting Detective Brady's quizzical gaze, I clarified, "Skippy is a Bullmastiff." Skippy dropped the ball at my feet and stared at Detective Brady.

"Really?" Detective Brady asked, eyeing Skippy critically. "Are you sure he's a purebred?"

"Yes," I said.

"Well, that's what his mother claims, anyway," Nigel added as he picked up the tennis ball and threw it down the hall. Skippy happily charged after it.

Officer Hax smothered a smile, while Detective Brady stared blankly at Nigel. "I'm assuming that you aren't here to discuss Skippy's pedigree," I said. "Have there been any developments as to who attacked our employee?'

Detective Brady returned his gaze to me. "Well, we have a few leads." He paused and began to lightly tap his forefinger on his pants leg. Officer Hax glanced over at him, her expression curious, but she said nothing. Officer Kelly said nothing either, but that was to be expected. The silence continued.

Over the years, I'd learned that some detectives preferred to dictate how an interview was conducted while others preferred for the witness to take the lead. The theory behind the latter was that a witness's questions could be just as informative as their answers. I was never a big fan of this technique. Detective Brady, however, apparently was. I smiled politely, sat back into the couch, and waited. Skippy bounded back with the ball and dropped it in Nigel's lap. He threw it again.

Detective Brady quietly drummed out a rhythm on his leg for a few more minutes before narrowing his eyes and asking, "You don't have any questions?"

"Oh, I have lots of questions," I assured him. "However, I assumed that you came here to *tell* us something. But, if you're trying to do so through Morse code, I should warn you that I'm a bit rusty on my dashes and dots."

Detective Brady blinked and abruptly stopped tapping his leg. "Yes. Well, we're pretty confident that whoever attacked your employee is also responsible for some recent break-ins in the area. No doubt the intruders assumed that your house was empty, and unfortunately, your employee must have gotten in the way."

I stared at Detective Brady. "I'm sorry, did you just say she must have 'gotten in the way'? You make it sound like she wandered out into traffic. You do realize she was beaten within an inch of her life?"

Detective Brady crossed his legs and fixed the crease on his pant leg before answering.

"I am familiar with all of the aspects of this case," he replied.

"Then I'm surprised that you think this was a break-in gone wrong," I replied. "The tapes were the only things taken."

"Which, I understand, are very valuable," he countered.

"So too is jewelry, TV sets, and stereos," I replied. "And yet none of those items were taken."

He aimed a condescending smile my way. "Yes, but they are much harder to carry. I think I have a pretty good handle on what happened here, Mrs. Martini. This area isn't immune to petty crimes. We suspect it's some local kids. They probably assumed the house was empty and were startled to find Ms. Evans in residence. They must have panicked and grabbed what was easy — namely the tapes. Pretty straightforward, really."

Skippy returned with the ball, this time dropping it in Officer Hax's lap. She obligingly tossed it down the hall.

"How do you figure that the thieves knew about the tapes in the first place?" I asked.

"I believe it's been a common topic in the local papers," Detective Brady replied.

"That's true," I conceded. "However, the papers only reported that the tapes were being edited at Nigel's office. Nothing was ever mentioned about us doing work on them here."

Skippy returned with the ball. He dropped it at Detective Brady's feet, where it stayed. "I imagine it was just a lucky break for whoever broke in," he said.

"I disagree," I said. "I think that whoever did this came here with the sole intent of taking those tapes. DeDee called my husband while we were at the Vanity Fair after party. It was clear from his side of the conversation that DeDee had discovered something important on the tapes."

Detective Brady arched a disbelieving eyebrow. "And what was this important discovery?" he asked Nigel. Skippy laid his massive head on Detective Brady's lap, his eyes pleading. Detective Brady ignored him.

"I don't know," Nigel said. "I couldn't hear her. I thought she was saying something about someone named Giuseppe."

"And do you know anyone named Giuseppe?" he asked.

"No," Nigel admitted.

Detective Brady smiled as if this proved his point. "And yet, you think that not only could someone else hear what you couldn't, but that it was important enough to come over here, break in, and attack a defenseless woman?" he asked. "Seems a bit silly."

"Seems a bit silly that you won't even consider it as a possibility," I countered.

Detective Hax began coughing into the crook of her arm. Detective Kelly stared at his shoes. Skippy admitted defeat. He removed his head from Detective Brady's lap and trotted off down the hall.

"Mrs. Martini," Detective Brady said, his voice growing annoyed, "I am sorry about the attack on your employee and the break-in. And I understand that you might be tempted to put your *former* skills to use in finding out who did this, but please let me handle this. I can assure you that the only crimes connected with the Vanity Fair Party, other than a few drunken antics and some very questionable attire, was the theft of an Oscar. All pretty standard stuff for that crowd. I deal with it every year."

"Someone stole an Oscar?" I asked.

He nodded. "Yes. Christina Franklin's. She reported it early this morning. It'll turn up. No doubt in James Franco's possession. That man has an odd sense of humor."

"Detective Brady, with all due respect," I began. He cut me off.

"*Mrs.* Martini, please. Are you seriously suggesting that someone who was at that party — a Hollywood A-Lister, no less —

broke into your house and attacked your employee?"

"Are you seriously suggesting that it's *not* a possibility?" I countered.

Detective Brady took a deep breath. "I appreciate your input," Mrs. Martini, "but I *think* I know what I'm doing."

I was about to answer to the contrary when Skippy came back into the room, carrying something in his mouth. Walking directly to Detective Brady, he then sat before him and dropped the object at his feet.

It was an Oscar statue. And based on the dried hair and blood that covered the pedestal, it also appeared to be the weapon used to attack DeDee.

Nigel crossed his leg and fixed an imaginary crease on his leg before saying, "Far be it from me to tell you how to do your job, Detective, but I *think* you might want to rethink that idea."

Skippy barked. I made a mental note to buy him a steak dinner.

Twenty-Four

Detective Brady left almost immediately, but not before he reminded me that I had no business "poking around in this case" and that he was more than capable of solving this without the help of a "bored housewife." Officers Hax and Kelly followed close behind. It might have been my imagination, but I think Officer Hax gave me a sympathetic smile on her way out.

I called Mandy and asked her if she knew anything about Christina's stolen Oscar. "No," she answered with a laugh. "But I doubt it's actually been stolen. This has happened before. They usually turn up in a few days with a couple of . . . ah, additions, if you know what I mean."

"No, I don't, nor do I want to," I said.

"Franco probably has it," Mandy said, "He loves to tweak Christina. I remember him saying something last year about . . ."

"Franco doesn't have it," I said, cutting

her off. "The police do."

"The police?" Mandy repeated. "Why do they have it?"

"We just gave it to them," I said. "Skippy found it."

"Skippy? How did he get it?" Mandy asked.

I quickly told her about the break-in and the attack on DeDee. Mandy gave a hiss of surprise. "Dear God," she said. "You can't really think that Christina attacked Dee?"

"I have no idea," I answered. "But I intend to find out. Do you know how I can get in touch with her? I have a few questions I'd like to ask her."

"Of course. I'll call her and have her contact you right away," she said.

"Thanks," I said. "And, Mandy, in the meantime? All of this is off the record, okay?"

"Of course, Nic. I didn't hear a word from you."

Christina called me five minutes after I hung up from Mandy. "Mandy told me what happened," she said her voice tight with emotion. "I'm horrified to think that my Oscar might have been used to hurt someone. I'd be glad to tell you what little I know, though. Why don't you and your husband come to my house for lunch this afternoon? Mandy is coming as well," she said.

"I don't want to put you out," I said.

"It's no trouble at all," Christina said, "and besides, the paparazzi have been all over me lately. I'd rather not go out."

I had just agreed when Christina surprised me by adding, "Oh, and Mandy says that you are to bring Skippy, but under no circumstances is Nigel allowed to bring Roscoe, whoever he is."

I stifled a laugh. "That shouldn't be a problem. I think Roscoe is in rehab anyway."

"Oh, I'm sorry to hear that," Christina said. "Is he a relative?"

"No, he's a foul-mouthed parrot," I answered.

"Oh," she said, slowly. "I see. Well, then I'm really sorry he can't make it."

Footage from the Set of *A Winter's Night* 5/5/96

Barry is sitting in his chair, making notes in a script. In the distance yelling can be heard. It is Frank Samuel. He is berating someone about a set mistake.

FRANK Are you a complete idiot or just a partial idiot? I can't tell. But let's see if we can't figure it out. In the nightclub scene, you have Hanna drinking a coke, right?
CREWMEMBER Yes, sir.
FRANK Well, not only do you have her drinking it directly from the bottle, which no well-bred lady would ever do, you screwed up the bottle. Care to tell me how you did this?

Barry looks up from his notes and turns his head to listen to the tirade. He closes his eyes with resigned frustration. After a second, he pulls out his cell phone and quickly dials a number.

FRANK I asked you a question! Look at the damn bottle and tell me what you see!

CREWMEMBER It . . . it says Coca-Cola, sir.

BARRY (speaking quietly into his phone) Z? Hey, it's Barry. Uh-huh. Yeah. He's at it again. I don't know, some poor bastard in props, I think. But it's only a matter of time before he heads my way, and I just can't deal with him today. (Pauses and laughs) I stand corrected. Wait a sec, Z.

Barry cocks his head to listen to Frank.

FRANK (his voice growing even louder and angrier) I can read, you idiot! Although, I have to admit, I'm mildly surprised that YOU can. The logo is painted in red paint!

CREWMEMBER Uh . . . you want it a different color?

FRANK No, I don't want it painted a different color, you moron! I don't want it painted at all! What year is this movie set in?

CREWMEMBER Uh . . . 1949?

BARRY (rubbing his hand over his face) Anyway, could you possibly . . . ? Thanks, Z. You're a lifesaver. A gorgeous lifesaver. (pauses) Yeah, I think she's around here somewhere. What? No, of course not!

Don't be silly. She's having a blast following John around, and God knows he'll never get sick of adoration. Yeah, right? Okay, see you in a few. Thanks, Z.

Barry hangs up the phone and looks over to where Frank is yelling.

FRANK That's right! 1949! And Coke didn't start painting its logo onto the bottles until 1957! So unless we've added a time travel element to this movie that I'm unaware of, you've got the wrong damn bottle! Where the hell is Barry? Barry! Where the hell are you?

Barry sighs and stands up. He puts down his script and begins to walk toward Frank's voice.

BARRY Over here, Frank.

Twenty-Five

A few hours later, Nigel, Skippy, and I were seated on the terrace of Christina's Malibu home drinking white wine and eating Salad Niçoise. Below us the Pacific Ocean lapped at the white sands of Zuma Beach. Above us, white puffs of clouds floated across the clear blue sky. Nigel said he felt like he was in an ad for anti-depressants.

In addition to Mandy, Sebastian and Janice had joined us for lunch. The former checked his emails on his phone while the latter idly read the local paper's coverage of the Oscars.

"So, when did you notice that your Oscar was missing?" I asked Christina.

She took a sip of her wine before answering. "It was when I was getting ready to leave, actually," she said. "Around one, I think?" She turned to Sebastian to corroborate this.

Still looking at his phone, Sebastian nodded and said, "One fifteen."

"Right," Christina said, "Anyway, I went to get my statue and realized it was gone. Of course, I didn't think anything of it at the time. Actually, I assumed Franco had it. Last year, he dressed up Meryl's as a Ken doll. But when I asked him, he swore he had nothing to do with it."

"Do you remember who else was there when you left?" I asked.

Christina's delicate brows pulled together as she tried to remember. "I remember seeing Frank and Barry," she said. "They were huddled together in a corner deep in conversation."

"What about Cecelia? Was she still there?" I asked, remembering her hope to leave early.

Christina shook her head. "No. About an hour or so earlier, she marched over to both of them and yelled something about them being ungallant pigs. She said she was going home."

"What did they say?"

Christina shrugged her shoulder. "Nothing really. Barry just waved her off, and Frank said something about making sure that Danielle got a ride."

"Did Cecelia seem upset?" I asked.

Christina considered the question for a

moment, and then said, "Not really. I mean, she was annoyed, yes, but she's used to Barry's ways by now. Once he gets into a business discussion, it's hard to pull him away."

"How do you know he and Frank were talking business?" I asked.

She looked at me in surprise. "Well, I guess I don't actually," she said slowly. "I just assumed. I mean, when the two of them get like that, it's usually about business."

I nodded. "So, once you discovered your statue was gone, did you call the police?" I asked.

Christina nodded. "Yes, but not until later. I honestly assumed that it was either a prank or that someone had taken mine home by mistake. At one point there were a bunch of them on our table."

"Do you remember whose?" I asked.

Christina frowned in concentration. "Well, there was Barry's and Frank's. And Meryl's and Tom's."

"But those are all accounted for?" Mandy asked.

Christina nodded. "Yes. And when no one came forward with mine, I called the police. I can't tell you how sick I am that someone used it to hurt your employee. How is she by the way?"

"She's doing better," I said, "Thank God. However, she has no memory of the attack."

"Do the doctors think that her memory will return?" Janice asked.

"They haven't said," I answered.

"I still can't wrap my head around the whole thing," said Christina. "I mean, I know people are excited to see those tapes, but to attack someone just to get them? It doesn't make sense."

"It doesn't," I agreed. "From what we've seen of the tapes so far, it all seems pretty banal. I was hoping that you might be able to shed some light as to why anyone would want to prevent us from publishing those tapes."

"I'll try. What do you need to know?" she asked.

"That's the problem. I don't know exactly," I said. "I'm just trying to get an idea of what it was like back then. What was the atmosphere on the set like? Was it tense?"

Christina sat back against the white cushions and crossed her long legs. "You haven't been on too many movie sets, have you?" she said with a small laugh. "There's *always* tension. But I'd say that *A Winter's Night* wasn't too bad." She glanced at Mandy. "You were on the set a fair amount. Did you think it was tense?"

Mandy rolled her eyes. "Well, not unless Frank was around. Then it was extremely tense."

Christina tipped her head in agreement. "That's true."

"Why was that?" I asked.

"I don't know. He was just a bundle of nerves then," Christina said with a shake of her head. "He was *always* underfoot, either suggesting ideas to Barry or worrying that we were over budget, or that we wouldn't finish in time. He drove Barry nuts. I remember one time the two of them got into a huge screaming match that culminated with Barry threatening to have him thrown off the set." Christina laughed. "God, I remember how Frank would stomp around the set breathing out of his nose like an angry bull." Turning to Sebastian, she said, "Bash, what was that nickname you gave him? He was the bull in the *Bugs Bunny* cartoon?"

"Toro," Sebastian said, still looking at his phone.

Christina smiled. "That's right! Toro. After every one of Frank's rants, Bash would mutter, "Of course you realize, this means war!"

Everyone laughed, except for Janice. "Well, I thought Frank behaved just fine on the set," she said. "He had a picture to make

— an important one — and he wanted it made right. Plus, he had invested a ton of his own money in the project. When you have that kind of responsibility on your shoulders, you have to be tough. Someone has to be the 'bad guy' or nothing will get done."

Mandy shook her head in disagreement. "With all due respect," she said, "The only reason anything got done on that set is because Zelda was around. She was the only one who could make Frank see reason."

"What was she like?" Nigel asked. "I've only seen a little of her on the footage."

"She was different," Christina said thoughtfully. "I mean, for this town. She was the type of person who really looked at you when you talked and actually listened. She didn't have a hidden agenda. She wasn't trying to get information out of you, or get you to pass on information to someone else. And she adored Danielle. I remember the two of them together on the set. They played this one card game all the time. I don't remember what it was, but they would both cheat so outrageously until they were crying with laughter." Christina's voice trailed off. Across from me, Janice's posture grew stiff and her lips pressed together.

Mandy nodded. "Zelda got along with

everybody. Especially Barry," she said with a smile. "He once told me that he had her number on speed dial for when Frank got out of hand. Barry would call Zelda; Zelda would then pay a surprise visit, during which she would somehow smooth things over and convince Frank to take a break."

Christina laughed. "Now that I think about it," she said, "Zelda did make a lot of 'sudden' appearances on the set. But she definitely could calm him down. It's funny. I thought Zelda and Frank were the perfect couple. I never thought they'd get divorced. I guess it just goes to show how naïve I was."

"You're not naïve," said Mandy. "Zelda *was* nice. Of all of Frank's wives, she was the best. He was an idiot to ever let her go. He may be a brilliant producer, but he's a complete jackass when it comes to women."

"Why did they get divorced?" I asked.

Mandy gave an airy wave with her hand. "Oh, you know — the usual reasons. He couldn't keep his damn zipper zipped. Ended up leaving her for some bimbo half his age and," seeing the pained look cross Christina's face, she stopped short. "Oh God, Christina," she gasped. "I'm so sorry! I'm such an ass. I didn't mean to . . ."

Christina took a deep breath and shook her head as if to negate Mandy's self-reprimand. "Please, don't worry about it. I'm fine," she said, her voice barely audible. With a bitter laugh, she added, "Hell, if everyone had to avoid referencing men who've left their wives for younger women, conversations in this town would come to a screeching halt."

"You're better off without him anyway," Janice said with a brisk dismissal. "But I still say you're wrong about Frank. He was no worse than any other producer with a movie to shoot. If he was hard on you, it was for a good reason. After all, you know what they say, 'You can't make an omelet without breaking a few eggs.' "

Sebastian looked up from his phone. "Is Christina the omelet or the egg?" he asked. "I can never remember."

Christina snorted. Janice shot her a derisive look. "Oh, please. What do you have to complain about?" she asked. "And in any case, I don't remember Frank and Barry fighting all that much, but even if they did, it's all forgotten now. They're obviously still good friends."

"Well, seeing how Barry is married to Frank's sister, it's in his best interest if he stays on good terms with Frank," observed Sebastian. "You don't want to get on the wrong side of a Samuel. They play for keeps.

If Frank or Cecelia ever turned their backs on him, Barry's egg wouldn't just be broken, it would be cooked."

"Speaking of bad eggs," said Janice, "The person you should be focusing on is Melanie Summers."

Sebastian stared at his mother in confusion. "Who the hell said anything about bad eggs?" he asked.

"You did," replied Janice.

"I said 'broken' not 'bad,' " Sebastian said.

Janice dismissed this with a flick of her wrist. "Broken. Bad. Same difference," she said.

"Not to the Board of Health," Nigel said.

"My point is," Janice continued, "Melanie Summers was a bad egg. A broken, bad egg."

Christina tensed. "Mother," she said in a low warning voice.

"Don't 'Mother' me," Janice said holding out her hand as if to stop Christina's words. "Now, I know there are some who say it's wrong to speak ill of the dead. . . ."

"Oh, I think I know the group you mean," Sebastian offered helpfully. "Polite society? Decent human beings?"

". . . but in her quest for stardom," Janice blithely continued, "Melanie Summers would do anything *or anyone.*" She paused and pursed her lips, "*If* you know what I mean."

Sebastian leaned forward, his expression earnest. "For the sake of argument, let's say we don't. Is there a specific book you might recommend? Maybe one with pictures?"

Christina leaned forward as well, her eyes bright. "Or even better, a movie?" she asked.

Janice ignored them both. "The sad fact is, Melanie Summers used sex to advance her career. And I'd imagine that there are some people in this town who would prefer for that fact to remain unknown."

"Are you seriously suggesting that Melanie was cast in leading roles because she slept with someone?" asked Mandy.

Janice gave a sanctimonious nod of her head. "The whole thing is disgusting."

"Look, I'll agree with you that Melanie wasn't a very nice person," Mandy said, "but she was a hell of an actress. I find it hard to believe that she got the lead in *A Winter's Night* because she slept with someone."

Janice only shrugged. "It's not for me to say," she said primly.

Christina stared at her mother. "For God's sake, Mother! You just did say it!"

"I never said who, and I never will. But it doesn't make it any less true," Janice replied.

A moment of confused silence followed. "You'll have to excuse my mother," Sebastian said looking at us apologetically. "She used to write assembly instructions for Ikea. She's not used to speaking clearly."

"Sebastian!" Janice protested. "That's not true at all. . . ." she said and then trailed off as she looked at the paper in her lap. Her mouth opened in surprise and then closed again. Glancing back up at us, she abruptly stood. "If you'll excuse me," she said with an excited tremor in her voice. "I need to make a phone call." Without another word, she turned and left.

FOOTAGE FROM THE SET OF *A WINTER'S NIGHT* 5/5/96

Barry sits in his chair. The set is mostly empty. He picks up his phone and dials a number.

BARRY Hey, CeCe, it's me. Yeah, I know, but I'm not going to be able to make it. I know, babe, I'm sorry. It's just Frank came tearing through here today and blew a gasket about some stupid prop. Huh? A Coke bottle. Yeah. I know. Anyway, Jeff and I are going to try and edit the scene if we can. Otherwise I'll have to reshoot it and that's going to set us back even further. Hmmm? I honestly don't know, but it could be a few hours. Yeah. I will. No, don't be silly. Go ahead without me. Yeah, I'm sure. Tell Dave and Macy that I'm sorry. Maybe try and set something up for next week. Okay. Okay. Yeah. I will. Okay. You too. Bye, doll.

Barry hangs up the phone. A minute later a

man walks by. He is casually dressed in jeans and a T-shirt.

BARRY (to the man) Hey, Jeff. Thanks for helping me reedit that scene today. Who knew a Coke bottle could cause so much grief?

JEFF Yeah, so much for having a Coke and a smile, eh?

BARRY You said it. Anyway, thanks. You saved my ass. Have a good night.

JEFF You too, Barry. See you tomorrow.

Jeff leaves. Barry waits a minute and then pulls out his phone and dials a number.

BARRY Hey, babe, it's me. Yep, all set. I'll be over in about fifteen, okay? (smiling) Yeah, me too.

He hangs up the phone.

Twenty-Six

"I wouldn't take what my mother says too seriously," Christina said with an apologetic smile. "As you could probably tell, she hated Melanie. Absolutely hated her. Melanie could be difficult at times, I grant you, but she wasn't a monster."

"Are you kidding me?" Mandy said in real surprise. "She was a first-class bitch! Why are you defending her?"

"I'm not defending her," Christina answered. "I'm just saying that she wasn't as bad as you're making her out to be."

"We are talking about Melanie Summers, correct?" Mandy asked.

Christina opened her mouth to reply but closed it when she noticed that her assistant had come out to the terrace. "Ms. Franklin," the woman said in a nervous voice, "I'm sorry to interrupt, but there's a detective here to see you. He says that it's important that he speak with you."

Christina's face paled and her eyes grew wide. She threw a worried glance at Sebastian who gave her a nod of reassurance. "Thank you, Ann," she finally said. "Please have him come out here."

Ann nodded and disappeared back into the house. Nigel and I took our cue to leave. "We should be going," I said. "Thank you again for lunch and for taking the time to talk to us."

"It was my pleasure, although I don't think I was of much help," Christina said, rising as well. "But please keep me posted on your employee."

"I definitely will," I said. Nigel and I said our good-byes and were heading back into the house when Detective Brady came out onto the patio. Seeing me, he came to a sudden stop. He did not appear happy to see me.

"Good afternoon, Detective Brady," I said with a smile. "How nice to see you again."

"I didn't know you were here," he said, his mouth pulling down into a frown.

"Well, we'll be sure to add that to the list," Nigel said, as he put his hand on the small of my back and began to steer me away.

"What's that supposed to mean?" Detective Brady demanded.

Nigel paused and glanced back over his

shoulder with a sigh. "Okay," he said in an indulgent tone, "We'll add that one too, but I've got to warn you — the list of things you don't know is getting pretty long."

Footage from the Set of *A Winter's Night* 5/7/96

Melanie is sitting at a table wearing a white robe. Her hair is arranged in a reverse roll. She is eating from what appears to be a cup of yogurt. Frank walks toward her, his expression one of forced joviality.

FRANK Well, there you are! How's my beautiful star today?

MELANIE (holding up the cup) "Well, I'm in the club!"

FRANK I understand you had a rough morning.

MELANIE I threw up, Frank. Actually, to be more specific, I threw up on *John.* How the hell do you think I am? I'll give you a hint, though. It ain't beautiful.

FRANK (faltering) Ahh, yes. I think I heard something about that.

MELANIE You *think* you heard something about that? Really, Frank? You're not sure? 'Cause, I got to tell you, if I heard about someone not only puking in front of the entire crew, but also all over her leading man, I *think* I might remember it. But then, I guess that's just me. I've always been pretty good about remembering things. I guess it's what makes me such a good actress.

FRANK You're upset.

MELANIE (laughing) Frank. Upset doesn't begin to even remotely cover it.

FRANK (soothingly) Well, I'm here to help. Tell me what I can do. You know I'll do anything for you.

MELANIE (stares at him for a beat) Really? Like what?

FRANK Come on, Melanie. I'm here for you. You know that. Tell me what you need so we can get you back to work. Remember, we have a picture to make. And this role, honey, it's going to put you back on top.

MELANIE (scoffs) Yeah, Frank. So you keep telling me. But if it's all the same to you, I'm not sure if I want to be back on top.

FRANK (indulgent tone) That's crazy talk. You've just got that stomach bug that's going around. Everything feels worse when you're sick. Take the rest of the day off, and I'm sure you'll feel better by tomorrow. These things usually run their course in twenty-four hours or so.

MELANIE Actually, Frank. There is something you can do for me.

FRANK (smiling) See? I knew I could help. Just name it.

MELANIE (turning her back to him) Don't let the door hit your ass on the way out.

Twenty-Seven

"Mr. Martini," I said, linking my arm through his, "I have a proposition for you."

"I'll do it," Nigel said immediately.

"Don't you want to hear what it is first?"

"Mother said never play hard to get."

I laughed. "Your mother said no such thing."

Nigel cocked his head. "You might be right about that. Now that I think about it, it was dark and I. . . ."

"Don't be ridiculous. I was going to suggest that you make me your dirtiest martini, we finish watching the tapes, and find what we're looking for."

"In the tapes or in the martinis?" he asked.

"Both if you're lucky," I answered.

Nigel grinned at me. "I do like the way you think, Mrs. Martini."

An hour later, Nigel and I were comfortably settled in our home office, with martinis, a remote, and notepad all within easy reach.

The footage was what you'd expect from a fourteen-year-old with her first handheld camcorder. There were a lot of jerky shots and segments when it was apparent that Danielle was looking at something with her own eyes and not through the camera lens. Not surprisingly, most of Danielle's footage was of John Cummings. There could be no doubt that she had a massive crush on the then twenty-three-year-old actor; she kept him in the focus of her lens as much as possible. It wasn't hard to see why. John was a good-looking man, but at age twenty-three he still had that non-threatening puppy-dog quality that made him a safe crush for teenage girls.

I was well into my second martini when Nigel picked up the remote and paused the tape. "You know what I think?" he said.

"What?"

"I think Melanie was pregnant."

"Because she threw up?"

"Well, that and what she just said to Frank. I don't think that's yogurt she's holding up there. I think it's pudding."

I frowned at him. "Pudding?"

He nodded. " 'In the pudding club' is slang for being pregnant. I think that's a cup of pudding Melanie is holding when she says, 'I'm in the club.' "

"Wait. It is? Seriously?"

He nodded again. "Seriously."

"Do I even want to know how you know that?" I asked.

"I was in the Hasty Pudding Club at Harvard. Among other things, I learned how to make a mean pot of hasty pudding." He paused and added, "Of course, my Spotted dick was something of a legend."

I shook my head. "I don't know why I always assume you're kidding."

I paused the tape and rewound it. "It seems someone else knew what it meant, too." I pointed to the figure just visible on the left side of the screen. Eyes round with understanding slowly morphed into an expression of furious disgust. Nigel sat back and looked at me with surprise. "Well, I'll be damned," he said with a low whistle.

"Probably," I agreed, leaning over and kissing him lightly on the mouth. "But first let's have dinner. How do omelets sound?"

"Sounds good to me."

"Good," I said. "I'll have mine with onions."

Nigel laughed. "Fine. I'll make you an omelet, but no onions."

I smiled at him. "Deal."

Twenty-Eight

We had just finished dinner when the phone rang. It was Mandy. Her voice was shaking.

"What's wrong?" I asked.

"That idiot detective is what's wrong," she said. "I think he thinks Christina attacked DeDee!"

"Why? What did he say?"

"Oh, nothing *specific,* but I could tell. You have to help her, Nic, I know Christina, and she wouldn't harm a fly."

"What do you want *me* to do?" I asked.

"I want you to help me prove that she didn't do it!" Mandy wailed.

I paused. "I don't think Detective Brady wants me involved."

"I don't give a rat's ass what that cheap suit wants!" Mandy exclaimed. "I *know* Christina is innocent. Please, Nic, you've got to help her. She's been through enough lately. This will kill her."

I refrained from pointing out that this was

an unlikely occurrence and asked, "What do you want me to do exactly?"

"I don't know! You're the detective!"

"Ex-detective," I corrected.

"Whatever. Just talk to people. See what you can find out."

I sighed before answering. "I'll see what I can do," I finally said. "But how do you propose I do this? I have no legal authority to just start interviewing people."

"I've already figured that part out," said Mandy. "I can get you to see whomever you need; starting tomorrow, in fact."

"What's tomorrow?" I asked.

"Barry is getting his Star on the Hollywood Walk of Fame. Afterward, the studio is throwing him a party downtown at the Beverly Wilshire Hotel. Everyone will be there. I already spoke with Barry, and he wants you and Nigel to come."

I considered the offer. "All right," I said. "We'll be there. Text me the details."

Mandy let out a sigh of relief. "Thanks, Nic. I owe you."

"Well, I want to find out who attacked DeDee, too. In the meantime, you might be able to help me find someone. Sara Taylor."

Mandy was quiet a moment. "Who?" she asked.

"Sara Taylor," I repeated. "Melanie Summers's personal assistant."

"Oh, that's right. Now I remember." She paused and then said, "I don't know where she is off the top of my head, but let me see what I can find out."

"Thanks, Mandy. I appreciate it."

"Are you kidding? I'm the one who should be grateful. Tell Nigel I'll give him and his parrot all the airtime he wants next year."

"If you're really grateful," I warned, "you'll do no such thing."

Within an hour, Mandy texted me Sara Taylor's address and the details about Barry's event. The former was still living in LA, not too far from us. Nigel called and introduced himself, saying that he needed to get her consent to publish the videos. She agreed, although reluctantly. We arranged to meet at her house around nine the following morning.

Nigel and I then retired for the night. In hindsight, it was a good idea to skip the onions.

Twenty-Nine

The next morning, Nigel insisted that Skippy accompany us, claiming that ever since the break-in he'd been skittish. "Are we talking about you or Skippy?" I'd asked. I was subsequently advised that I was unattractive when I was snide.

For the most part, I have gotten used to the stares Nigel and I receive when we go out with Skippy. It's the ones we get when we take him out in the car that are a little harder to adjust to. Nigel drives a cream-colored vintage 1968 DB6 Aston Martin convertible. When Skippy sits in the back, we appear to be a parade float that has drifted off course.

Sara Taylor lived a few miles north of downtown LA in a remodeled Venice Craftsman bungalow in the affluent beachside community of Marina del Rey. We left Skippy happily curled up on the backseat and made our way to the door. Our knock was promptly answered by a woman who bore little resemblance to the one on the tapes. Gone was the woman who hid in drab, shapeless outfits. This Sara was slim and fashionably dressed. Her long caramel-colored hair was expertly highlighted and hung in soft curls over her shoulders. Large blue eyes regarded us without the aid of thick glasses. Quiet confidence had replaced the nervous tension I'd witnessed on the tapes.

"You must be Nigel and Nicole Martini," she said with a gracious smile. "It's lovely to meet you. Won't you please come in?"

We followed her through a comfortable living room with wainscoting boxed ceilings, beadboard wall coverings, all tastefully decorated in various hues of blue and cream. From there we walked out onto the private back patio. Nigel and I sat on a cushioned wicker loveseat and accepted Sara's offer of coffee. "You have a lovely house, Ms. Taylor," I said.

"Please, call me Sara. But thank you," she said as she poured out three cups of coffee.

"How long have you lived here?" asked Nigel, as he accepted his cup.

"Oh, I guess it's close to seventeen years now," she said.

"Do you still work in Hollywood?" I asked.

Sara took a sip of her coffee and shook her head. "No. After Melanie's death, I guess you could say I lost my taste for the film industry. It destroys too many lives."

"I see." I said as I glanced around the plush surroundings. "Well, you certainly seem to be the exception to that rule."

A wary look crept in her eyes. "Melanie left me a little bit of money in her will. I made some wise investments and they paid off." She put her coffee cup down on the table with a decided clank. "You mentioned something about paperwork on the phone . . . ?" she prompted.

"Oh, yes," said Nigel. "It's just a standard release form giving us permission to use your image. Obviously, we won't include any footage that could prove embarrassing."

Sara raised an eyebrow. "I don't recall doing anything embarrassing."

"Oh, no, of course you didn't," Nigel said easily. "I meant that more as a universal term; not in regards to you."

She smiled slowly. "I see. Well then from what I can remember, you may find yourself having to cut out a lot."

Nigel flashed his most engaging smile. "Yes. There does seem to have been a certain amount of . . . shall we say 'tension' among certain people on the set?"

Sara nodded. "Yes, I believe it would be safe to say that. Hollywood egos are a breed unto themselves."

"Melanie and John Cummings seemed to especially butt heads," I said.

Sara laughed softly. "They certainly did," she agreed. "But that was them. Fire and Ice, I used to call them. To them, fighting was a kind of foreplay."

"So, you think that they would have gotten back together had Melanie not died?" I asked surprised.

Sara gave an adamant nod. "Without a doubt. It was just a matter of time."

"But from the footage, it seemed that Johnny had moved on and was with Christina Franklin," I said.

Sara shrugged. "He wouldn't have stayed. Not while Melanie was still around. She was in his blood. It was as simple as that. Those two couldn't stay away from each other if they tried."

"It sounds like you knew her very well," I said. "How long did you work for her?"

Sara paused. "Seven years," she said quietly.

"I'm sorry if we're bringing up a painful subject," Nigel began, but Sara waved him off.

"No, it's fine," she said. "It was difficult

for me at the time, of course. We'd been quite close in our own way."

"Did you have any idea that she was using drugs again?" I asked.

Sara shook her head. "None at all. I was as surprised as anyone. I really thought she'd beaten it." She idly swirled her coffee with her spoon.

"From the footage we've seen, it appeared that she wasn't feeling well," I said.

Sara stopped swirling her spoon and glanced up at me. "What do you mean?" she asked.

"Nothing," I replied. "I just noticed that Melanie was sick to her stomach a few times."

"Was she? I don't really remember. It was so long ago." Lifting the silver coffee urn, she asked. "Would you like more coffee?"

"Yes, please," I answered, holding out my cup for her to fill.

As Sara poured I said, "It almost seems like she was coming down with something or maybe she was . . ."

Hot coffee spilled on my wrist. "Oh, I'm so sorry!" Sara said as she put down the urn. Handing me a napkin, she added, "I can be so clumsy at times. Did I burn you?"

"Not at all," I said, taking the napkin. "I'm fine."

"Oh, I know what you're thinking about," Nigel said to me. "Wasn't Melanie allergic to fish or something? Didn't she have a reaction?"

Sara's face cleared. "Oh, yes! That's right! Now I remember. She ate a salad that turned out to have been made with lobster in the dressing. Poor thing was horribly allergic to shellfish. She'd break out in hives, which as you can probably understand isn't optimal when you're in the middle of making a movie."

"No, I imagine not," I said.

Sara took a sip of her coffee. "That's why I always made sure I had an EpiPen on the set. You never knew what you were going to get from the craft table."

I stared at her. Nigel opened his mouth, but I stepped on his foot. Hard. Thankfully he took my meaning and said nothing.

THIRTY

"DeDee wasn't saying 'Giuseppe'!" I said to Nigel after we'd left and we were back in the car. "She was saying 'EpiPen'!"

"Yeah. I got that," he said. "And you're throwing out those damn shoes the second we get home. What the hell are they made of anyway?"

"Steel, naturally."

"Naturally."

"Well, you have to admit," I said, "this certainly changes things."

"Are we talking about your shoes or Melanie's death?" Nigel asked, as he pulled onto the highway. A trucker honked his horn and waved at Skippy.

"Melanie's death," I answered. "Someone must have tampered with the EpiPen knowing that Melanie was going to need it."

Nigel shook his head in disgust. "That's what DeDee must have seen and was trying to tell me. And I helpfully shouted it out for everyone to hear."

I reached over and squeezed his hand. "This is not your fault, Nigel," I said firmly. "You had no idea what DeDee was saying, let alone that it could endanger her."

Nigel fell silent and concentrated on driving. After a minute he asked, "Do you think whoever tampered with the pen was the father of Melanie's baby?"

"It's possible," I answered.

"Sara was really trying to sell us the idea that Melanie and John were going to get back together," Nigel said. "Do you think there's any truth to that?"

"I'm not sure," I admitted. "There's certainly nothing on the tapes to support that, but that isn't proof. I do think Sara is hiding *something.* When I first asked her about Melanie being ill, she claimed it was too long ago to remember. And yet in the next breath she was telling us about the ingredients in a salad dressing."

"I caught that," Nigel said. "Do you think she's hiding the identity of the father? Could he be the source of her wise investments?"

"I think it's a distinct possibility."

Thirty-One

The Hollywood Handprint and Footprint ceremonies are held outside the famed Grauman's Chinese Theater. Tourists love them because they're free to the public, and you never know who you might see there. Today's crowd had lucked out. Barry had brought along Frank, Christina, and John, who in turn each stood up and gave a short speech. The paparazzi were having a field day. Mandy had gotten us VIP passes so we were able to watch the ceremony up close. Unfortunately, this resulted in the addition of a certain dog's paw prints finding their way into Barry's cement block. I was mortified, but Barry only laughed and said, "Leave it. People always say I'm a son of a bitch, anyway. Let them think they're right!"

After the ceremony, we headed over to the rooftop of the Beverly Wilshire Hotel. A sleek and modern terrace with a panoramic view of the city, the spot was a favorite among Hollywood's elite. Striped cabana-like booths and canary yellow umbrellas surrounded a crystal blue wadding pool. In the distance the iconic Hollywood sign stood proud. Against all this, upwards of one hundred of Barry's closest friends mingled. Janice saw us first and came over immediately. "Nigel and Nic! How lovely to see you again," she gushed. Based on her overly friendly greeting, I suspected that she knew why we'd been asked to come. "I'm so pleased that you could join us!" Looking down at Skippy, she added, "And *this* precious boy must be Skippy."

Skippy cocked his head and studied Janice. From his expression, I don't think he liked being referred to as a "precious." Still, he sat and politely offered her his paw. Janice cooed over him as if he had addressed her in fluent French. "Well, isn't he the *sweetest* thing?" she said clapping her hands.

As there was no polite way to ask if she'd been drinking, I said nothing. Janice escorted us to where Christina and Mandy stood talking, their heads pressed close together. "Darling!" she sang out as she approached, "Nic and Nigel are here!"

At the sound of her mother's voice, Christina's head snapped up. An expression of irritation flickered across her face as she regarded Janice. Ignoring her mother completely, Christina greeted us with a grateful smile.

"Nic. Nigel," she said extending her hands toward us. "Thank you so much for coming."

"Thank you for inviting us," I answered.

"Well, I'll let you talk," Janice said with a bright smile. "But, Christina, don't neglect Frank. Remember, he's getting ready to make his casting decision, and I've got a really good feeling that he's going to pick you. It never hurts to spread a little extra sunshine his way, if you know what I mean."

"Go away, Mother," Christina said closing her eyes.

Surprisingly, Janice did not take offense at her daughter's dismissal. Instead, she let out a little laugh and patted Christina on the arm. "You always get grouchy when you don't eat. I'll fix you a plate of something. Veggies, I think. If Frank gives you that role, which I'm sure he will, you'll have to slim down."

"Go away *now,* Mother," Christina repeated.

Janice merely tittered, shaking her head as she moved away. Mandy looked askance at Christina, "Is she drunk?" she asked.

Christina shrugged. "Probably. She's sure that Frank is going to offer me the role in Barry's new film. She's been celebrating."

"I thought the studio hadn't signed off on that yet," Mandy said.

Christina looked at her sharply. "Where did you hear that?" she asked.

Mandy's gaze slid away. "Barry might have mentioned it to me in passing," she admitted.

Christina's lips pursed together. "Perfect." Taking a deep breath, she said, "You know what? Who gives a damn? I've got bigger things to deal with." She took a deep breath and turned to Nigel. "I can't tell you how much it means to me that you came, especially in light of what that horrible detective seems to think about me," she said looking up at him. "But, I hope you'll believe me when I tell you that I had absolutely *nothing* to do with the attack on DeDee."

Her voice shook slightly as she spoke; it was a nice touch. "Of course you didn't," Nigel said with a reassuring smile.

"I'd like to do whatever I can to help you find who did do it, though," she said, placing her hand on Nigel's arm. "I know it's silly, but I feel partly responsible; after all it was *my* Oscar that they used in the attack."

Nigel covered her hand with his and patted it. "It's kind of you to offer," he said. "But you'll be happy to hear that Nic made some progress today. We met with Sara Taylor this morning."

Christina frowned. "Sara Taylor?" she repeated.

"Melanie Summers's old personal assistant," I explained. "It was Mandy who was able to track her down for us, actually," I added with a nod toward Mandy.

Christina glanced quickly at Mandy and removed her hand from Nigel's arm. "Oh. I see. Oh, yes. *Sara.* I remember her now," she said. "Quiet girl. I didn't envy her job. Melanie wasn't an easy woman to work for."

"How is Sara?" Mandy asked.

"Well, I didn't know her from before, of course," I said, "but she seems to be doing quite well for herself."

"Is she still an assistant?" Christina asked.

"No," I said. "She said she retired from the business soon after Melanie died. She bought a house out in Marina Del Rey."

Mandy arched an eyebrow at this. "Nice area," she said.

"She said something about having made some wise investments," I answered, just as Sebastian approached. He nudged Christina's arm slightly, as if to get her attention. Christina's drink slipped from her hand and spilled down her front.

"Sebastian!" she cried. "You big oaf. Look what you've done!"

Sebastian glanced down at his sister in surprise. "What did I do?" he asked in confusion.

"You spilled my drink," she answered, indicating her now wet skirt.

"I barely touched you," he protested.

"Then why am I wet?" she retorted. "If you'll excuse me," she said to the rest of us, "I need to mop this off me. I'll be right back."

Sebastian watched her march off with an expression of surprise. Turning to Mandy, he asked, "What was that all about?"

Mandy shrugged and took a sip of her wine. "She's a little on edge. On top of everything else, your mother has been at her about Frank's new movie. She told her to 'play nice,' " Mandy said bending her fingers into air quotes.

Sebastian made a noise of disgust. "God, some things never change."

"Which project is this?" Nigel asked.

"It's a courthouse drama set in the south about a judge who becomes romantically involved with the prosecutor," said Sebastian. "Christina is being considered for the role of the prosecutor, but the studio is concerned that she's too old for the part. The kicker, of course, is that Johnny has been cast as the judge."

Mandy rolled her eyes in disgust. "Typical Hollywood sexism. And you know what's worse?" she asked before answering her own question. "Barry says the studio wants to give the role to Jules." She tilted her head to an area to our right. Looking over I saw Jules. She was standing at the edge of the pool, her body pressed close to Frank's. He said something, and she giggled and patted his arm.

"Ouch," I remarked.

Mandy nodded. "Ouch, is right."

"What the hell is Jules doing?" Sebastian asked.

"The only thing she knows how to do," Mandy said. "Playing nice."

Sebastian frowned and watched the pair with narrowed eyes.

THIRTY-TWO

Mandy and I had gone inside the restaurant in search of a restroom, when we bumped into John. He was talking to two very pretty and very young women. One was blonde; the other was brunette. Other than that, there was little to set them apart. "Hello, John. Enjoying yourself?" Mandy asked archly.

John turned bleary eyes in her direction and produced a lopsided smile. "Mandy!" he cried, either oblivious or indifferent to her annoyance. "How are you? I want you to meet my new friends."

"Oh, gosh. How can I say this?" Mandy asked as if at a loss for words. Then, with a snap of her fingers she said, "Oh, right. I'd rather not."

John ignored her. Waving his hand toward the girls, he said, "This is Jasmine and Stacy." It wasn't clear who was who. However, it wasn't an omission that was likely to plague me. "Girls, you know Mandy," John continued before gesturing toward me. "And this is Nicole Martini. You know, the one with the tapes everyone is talking about."

The blonde gave me a sympathetic frown. "Did that happen to you, too? God. Don't you hate it when guys film you and put it on the Internet?" she asked.

The brunette snickered and punched her friend in the arm. "You idiot!" she giggled. "Not *those* kind of tapes. He's talking about those old *movie* tapes. You know, the ones of that famous movie." She paused a moment mentally searching for the name, before going with, "Whatchamacallit."

"Also known as *A Winter's Night,*" I said.

The brunette nodded and smiled at me as if I'd said something clever. "That's the one!"

"Oh!" said the blonde, her eyes going wide. Turning to John, she put her hand on his arm. "You were in that movie! But, wait." Her brow creased in thought. "Didn't somebody die on that set?" she asked.

John stiffened. "Yes," he said, his voice going flat. "Melanie Summers."

"I heard Barry Meagher was having an affair with her," the brunette said, her voice barely a whisper.

The blonde giggled. "Big deal. Barry Meagher has an affair with *everyone,*" she said.

Next to me Mandy froze. "What did you just say?" she asked, her voice low and angry.

The blonde seemed surprised at the question. Opening her vapid brown eyes very big, she said, "Oh come on, everyone knows that Barry is a total man slut. I mean, don't get me wrong. The man exudes sex appeal. He may be old, but he's still got it. Hell, I wouldn't say no to a private meeting with him, if you know what I mean."

Mandy glared at the woman, mouth pinched, nose flared. Leveling John with a glacial stare, she hissed, "Get your little friends out of here, *now.* I doubt their future holds more promise than a short stint at Hooters and a lifetime on Z-Paks but Cecelia will destroy you and them if she gets wind of this crap. This is a party for *Barry.* You'd do well to remember that."

The warning seemed to sober John. He nodded at Mandy and began to usher the protesting girls outside. Mandy watched them go, her expression still furious. Once they were out of sight, she closed her eyes and took a deep breath. "You okay?" I asked after a minute.

She nodded and took another deep breath before opening her eyes. Shooting me an apologetic smile, she said, "Sorry. I just get so sick of those rumors. I feel so sorry for Cecelia. People have been saying their marriage is a sham since day one. They never had any kids, you know, which only added fuel to the fire. Everyone thinks Barry married her because she was Frank's sister and it would help his career."

"Did he?"

"Oh, absolutely," Mandy replied matter-of-factly. "But I still feel bad for Cecelia that everyone knows it."

We returned to the rooftop to find Christina, Janice, and Sebastian chatting with Danielle about living with her mother in Italy. "Bellagio is gorgeous," Danielle was saying. "In the mornings, Mom and I would sit on the patio and drink coffee and watch the mist float over Lake Como."

"It sounds perfect," said Christina.

"It was," Danielle said. She paused and added, "Well, it *almost* was. Not being able to see my dad every day was hard. I really missed him. I think my mom did, too. I don't think she ever got over him. After she died, I thought about staying in Bellagio, but it wouldn't be the same. Too many memories, I guess. Besides, it was time for me to come home."

"Your mom sounds like she was a very special lady," I said. "I've heard nothing but nice things about her from everyone. Which, as you probably know, is a rarity in this town."

Danielle looked at the floor and nodded. "Thank you. She *was* special." She paused and added, "But I've got my dad, and he's great, too.

"You're working for him as an editor now, right?" I asked. "Are you enjoying it?"

She nodded, a genuine smile lighting up her face. "I am. I absolutely love it. I always wanted to work in this business. The fact that I get to do so with my dad just makes it all the more amazing."

"Well, it seems like you have an eye for it. Even as a kid. You captured a lot of great things on your videos," I said.

Danielle looked at me with a doubtful smile and said, "I have a feeling you are being very polite. But thank you. Honestly, I had forgotten all about those tapes. I'm dying to watch them. When do you think they'll be ready?"

"I'm not sure, actually," I answered. "As you may have heard, we've hit a few bumps."

Her eyes widened with sympathy. "I did. I can't believe someone broke into your house," she said. "Do the police have any leads?"

I shook my head. "A few, but nothing solid yet," I answered.

"What are we talking about?" asked Jules in a sing-songy voice as she and Frank joined our group. She was wearing a skin-tight rose-colored sheath and had draped herself around Frank like a spring accessory.

"The latest on our break-in," I explained.

"Oh, that's right. I heard your employee was attacked," Jules said to Nigel, her eyes wide with concern. "Is that true?"

"It is," he said.

Jules's expression of concern quickly morphed into one of disgust. "How awful," she said. "I hope she is okay."

"That's kind of you," Nigel said.

Jules made a production of shaking her head as if she were lamenting the moral erosion of today's society. She really was a terrible actress. After a moment, she made a small noise as if startled by a sudden thought. "Correct me if I'm wrong," she said, "but didn't I hear something about an Oscar statue being used in the attack?" Across from me, Christina watched Jules with narrowed eyes.

"I don't know," Nigel answered amiably,

"Did you?"

Jules scrunched her face into an expression of serious concentration. After a minute, she looked up as if the answer had suddenly made itself clear. "Yes," she said. "I did. I'm sure of it." With a startled gasp, she then turned to Christina. "Didn't I hear something recently about *your* Oscar going missing?"

Christina took a steadying breath. "I don't know, Jules," she said. "I'm not an audiologist."

This time Jules's expression of confusion was genuine. "What?" she asked.

"I'm not an audiologist," Christina repeated as if she were talking to a deaf relative. She paused. "That's a doctor who checks your hearing," she explained slowly. "You seem concerned about yours, so maybe you should make an appointment."

Jules's mouth flattened into a thin glossy pink line. She squared her shoulders. Running her hand up to her hair, she then casually twirled a blonde lock of it around her right forefinger. "Maybe you're right," she said with a delicate shrug. "I have heard some strange things."

"Not unusual when one is a psychopath," agreed Sebastian to no one in particular.

"There are just so many *vile* rumors in

Hollywood," continued Jules, in a sorrowful voice. "Strange how many of them turn out to be true."

"Like the one that claims you can't act?" asked Sebastian.

Jules narrowed her eyes. "No," she snapped. "Like the one that claims that Melanie Summers's death wasn't an accident at all." She paused and then looked pointedly at Christina. "Funny how well her death worked out for you, *Christina,*" she said with an icy smile. "After all, it got you your big break, didn't it?"

Christina's face blanched. "Just what the hell do you mean by that?" she hissed through gritted teeth.

Jules opened her blue eyes very big and attempted to look surprised. She failed. "Why nothing at all, of course," she said.

Before Christina could respond, Janice stepped next to Jules, a bright smile pasted on her face. Lightly placing her hand on Jules's arm, she leaned her head in close. To anyone watching, it looked like nothing more than two friends sharing a quick chat. However, Janice's words, while delivered in a pleasant tone, were anything but friendly. "Listen to me, you two-bit hussy," Janice said, her mouth still stretched in a smile. "My daughter had nothing to do with Melanie's overdose. Do you hear me? *Nothing!* But I swear to God, if I *ever* hear you say anything like that again, I'll knock you on your backside so fast you'll think you're back at your first casting call!"

Jules took a step back and glared at Janice. Janice took another step forward, still smiling that unnerving blank smile. I really couldn't blame Jules for taking another step back. Of course, it was this last step that landed her squarely in the pool.

Thirty-Three

Once Jules hit the water, all hell broke lose. She flailed about in the deep end and let loose a rather impressive assortment of expletives. Skippy seemed to think it was a game and jumped in with her. This, however, only increased her screaming. By the time we'd extracted both of them from the pool, half of the guests were wet either from Jules's splashes or Skippy's post-pool fur shake. Nigel and I decided it was a good time to say our good-byes. No one put up much of an argument.

"I smell like a wet dog, and I have a headache," Nigel said, as we waited for the valet to bring our car.

"Poor baby. Come on, I know what will make you feel better."

"So do I," he said. "But you said we weren't allowed to do that in the car anymore."

I lightly slapped his arm. "That's not what

I meant. I'll order us some Chinese food and give you a neck massage. You'll feel better in no time."

Nigel pulled me close and kissed the top of my head. "Well, it'll never be as fun as the car, but okay."

Two hours later, Nigel, Skippy, and I were curled up together on the bed surrounded by half-empty take-out cartons. We had taken a break from watching the tapes and had stumbled across a *Breaking Bad* marathon. We were enjoying Walter White's descent into evil when Nigel suddenly sat up. "That's Mr. Luiz," he said, pointing at the TV.

I looked at the screen. Walter White was ringing up a customer at his car wash. "Who's Mr. Luiz? The customer?" I asked.

Nigel nodded. "The reporter at the Oscars — the one who wanted to buy the tapes. That's him. I'm sure of it."

I looked at the screen again. Nigel was right. It was the same man — or at least a younger, better-dressed version of him. "I suppose I should call Detective Brady," I said, as I reached for my phone. "Although, I doubt he's going to want to talk to me."

Not surprisingly, my call went to voice mail. I didn't really care, actually. I just wanted to be able to say that I had tried to get in touch with him. Besides, I didn't need Detective Brady's help in locating Mr. Luiz. I had Nigel for that.

THIRTY-FOUR

By late afternoon the next day, Nigel had tracked down the information we needed. The credits had listed the man at the car wash (a.k.a. David Luiz) as Tom Jacobs. Nigel made a few phone calls and finally got in touch with his agent. In no time at all, Nigel learned that Tom worked at a bar called The Wee Small Hours when he wasn't acting. When I asked him how he managed to get all this information, Nigel shrugged and said, "I may have mentioned something about a new reality show that followed men of a certain age still hoping for their big acting break."

"Nicely done, Mr. Martini," I said. "I believe that kind of detective work deserves to be rewarded."

"And being the clever detective that I am," he said with a grin, "I'm going to guess that my reward is a drink at The Wee Small Hours."

I tipped my head in consideration. "Actually, it's not," I said. "But if you want to go there after, we can do that too."

Nigel said that he was fine with that plan.

Around nine, Nigel and I slid into two empty stools at the Art Deco-inspired lounge. Dark paneling covered the walls, the bar itself was a sheath of glossy mahogany, and the stools were upholstered in red leather. Given the name of the place, I wasn't surprised to hear Sinatra belting out *Come Fly with Me* from the hidden speakers.

Tom was chatting with another patron. While I waited for him to notice us, I studied him. His hair was no longer gray, his glasses were gone, and his complexion was now clear, but it was our Mr. Luiz. When he finally turned to us, his eyes widened in surprise, and his lips pressed together tightly. An expression of indecision flitted across his face. Pulling his shoulders back, he walked toward us with brisk efficiency. "Evening, folks," he said with a cheerful smile, "What can I get you?"

"Two dirty Martinis," Nigel answered. Tom ducked his head in acknowledgement and set out to make the drinks. A few minutes later, he placed two glasses in front of us.

"Thank you," said Nigel. "You know, you look familiar. Have we met before?"

Tom smiled and shook his head. "I don't think so, but I am an actor. You might have seen me on TV."

"Maybe," Nigel said, taking a sip of his martini. "But for some reason I think we've actually met. Wait, I know — at the Oscars. Didn't we meet at the Oscars?"

Tom smiled as if he found the idea amusing. "I wish! Maybe one day, though. Fingers crossed and all that."

Nigel turned to me and asked, "Doesn't he look like that reporter we met? The one who wanted the tapes?"

I propped my elbows on the bar top and made a show of studying his face. Tom glanced away on the pretense of checking on the other customers. "He does," I finally said. "It's uncanny, actually."

"I guess I have a twin then," Tom said with a shrug. "What do they call those things that look just like you?"

"I think they're called twins," Nigel said.

"No, you know what I mean," said Tom. "People who look just like you, but aren't related to you," he explained. "What's that called?"

"A Jerry Springer episode?" Nigel offered.

"I think he means doppelganger," I said.

Tom snapped his fingers and smiled at me. "That's it! I guess I have a doppelganger," he said.

Nigel pretended to consider the idea. "I suppose that could be it," he said doubtfully, "but the resemblance is uncanny."

I nodded in agreement as I stared at Tom's face. "It is. I mean his hair is different and he's not wearing glasses," I said, "but other than that they're the same. Especially their complexions."

"My complexion isn't pockmarked!" Tom protested and then stopped himself.

I smiled and took a sip of my martini. "Never underestimate an actor's ego, Tom," I said.

Nigel laughed. "Nicely done, Mrs. Martini," he said clinking his glass against mine. "Once again I bow to your detective skills."

Tom's eyes grew wide. "You're a detective?" he asked.

"Is that a problem?" I asked him.

Tom glanced around the bar to see if anyone was listening. "Listen, it was just a job," he said in a low voice. "I didn't do anything illegal. I checked."

"Well, I'm not so sure about that," I said. "But why don't you tell me what your job *was* exactly."

Tom sighed. "I was to introduce myself to

you and tell you that I had a client who wanted to buy the tapes. I was given a foreign press pass so I could talk to you on the Red Carpet. Mr. Luiz was my own creation," he added proudly.

"And then what?" I asked.

Tom glanced at me in surprise. "And then, nothing. That was it. I was to tell you about the offer and give you the card. Did you call the number on the card?" he asked.

Nigel shook his head. "No. I gave it to the police, actually."

Tom swallowed a mouthful of air. "Why . . . why would you do that?" he asked.

"The night you offered to buy the tapes from us, our house was broken into and some of the tapes were stolen. Not only that, but our employee was viciously attacked. She's still in the hospital."

Tom's eyes grew wide. "I had nothing to do with that!" he said. "I swear!"

"I don't know, Tom," I said. "It doesn't look good."

"I swear I didn't! What can I do to prove it?" he asked.

"Well, for starters, you could tell us who hired you," I said.

Tom didn't even pause. "Mandy Reynolds," he blurted out.

I glanced at Nigel in surprise. "Mandy?" I repeated. "Did she say why?"

Tom shook his head. "No," he said. "She just said to approach you, make an offer, and give you the card."

"Whose number was on the card?" I asked.

He shook his head. "I don't know. Mandy set that up as well. If you called it, she'd contact me, and I'd become Mr. Luiz again and handle the sale." He closed his eyes and sighed. "I knew it. Damn it, I knew I shouldn't have taken the job. I just really needed the money. The competition is pretty stiff out there for guys like me."

"I imagine it is," Nigel agreed.

"But I promised myself that I'd give it a fair shot. I figure that if I can't make it after fifteen years, then I'll throw in the towel."

"How long have you been out here?" I asked.

"It'll be fifteen years this July," he answered.

Nigel stood up and threw some cash on the bar. "Well, Tom, I wish you all the best."

Tom eyed Nigel. "Hey, you're in the movie business, right?" he asked.

"In a way," Nigel answered. "Why?"

"Think you could give me any advice?"

Nigel drained the rest of his martini and

set the glass on the bar. “Sure. Use less vermouth.”

Footage from the Set of *A Winter's Tale* 5/5/96

John and Melanie are quietly running through their lines in a corner. Barry is sitting at a table drinking a cup of coffee and making notes on a script copy. Next to him sits a very pretty blonde. It is Mandy Reynolds. She is young — about twenty-four — and is wearing a short denim skirt and a blue blouse. Her long hair is pulled back into a low ponytail.

MANDY (looking over at John and Melanie) So, how are your co-stars doing today? Any bloodshed?

BARRY Not yet. But then again, it's early. Give them time.

MANDY I don't get the animosity. This time last year, they were madly in love. Now they despise each other. What happened?

BARRY (laughing) You really are new to Hollywood, aren't you? Well, the short story is that John got tired of living in Melanie's shadow, and Melanie believes that John arranged her stint in rehab to further his career at the expense of hers.

MANDY What's the long story?

BARRY Basically the same thing, but with some drug abuse, affairs, immaturity, and domestic battery. Mainly on Melanie's side.

MANDY Seriously? Any of it true?

BARRY (shrugging) Who knows? Melanie was a train wreck. There's no doubt that she needed rehab. But sometimes I wonder if John didn't use the whole sad affair as an excuse to step out of her shadow and into his own limelight.

MANDY (keeping her focus on Melanie) Well, she definitely looks better. Her color's back, and she's gained some weight back, but . . . I don't know, she looks tired.

BARRY (glancing up) Does she? I guess she does a little. But then again, we probably all do. Frank has been breathing down my neck day and night about every little thing. He's practically manic.

MANDY Really? Any idea why?

BARRY You mean other than the fact that he's a control freak and a jackass?

MANDY (laughing) And all this time, I thought in addition to being his brother-in-law, you were also really good friends.

BARRY We are. Which is why I didn't call

him an egomaniac prone to irrational and verbally abusive psychotic episodes.

MANDY Ahhh. Now I see the loyalty.

BARRY (smiling) That's off the record, by the way.

MANDY Which part?

BARRY (winking) All of it.

MANDY (smiling) That's too bad. You make for good copy.

BARRY (laughing) Ah, the story of my life.

MANDY Don't let the feminine exterior fool you, Barry. I'm a reporter first.

BARRY (pretending to be confused) Wait? You're a woman?

MANDY Well, thank you for your time, Mr. Meagher. Do you know if Ms. Franklin is on set? I'm scheduled to meet with her as well.

BARRY (frowning) What?

MANDY (smiling at something behind Barry) Oh, hello, Mrs. Meagher. How are you? I was just trying to find Christina for an interview. Did you happen to see her on your way in here?

Barry turns around in his seat. He sees a woman of about thirty-five approaching. She is plump, with a round pleasant face. It is Cecelia Meagher, Barry's wife.

CECELIA No, I don't think I did. Sorry. I did happen to see her mother, though. Nasty woman. (To Barry) She demanded — actually demanded — that I talk to you about giving Christina more screen time.

BARRY (shaking his head in annoyance) Well, you're in good company. She's been pestering everyone about that. The other day she even cornered one of the construction grips. Poor man didn't speak a word of English, which now that I think about it was actually a blessing.

CECELIA I know Janice has always been pushy, but she seems to have put the whole stage monster thing into overdrive lately. What's her problem?

BARRY To adequately answer that could take years, so I'll just skip to this week's problem. Janice claims that there's some secret conspiracy to give Melanie as much screen time as possible — at the expense of the rest of the actors' roles — but Christina's in particular.

CECELIA (pausing a beat) Is there?

BARRY Of course not! God. Step away from the Kool-Aid, CeCe. It's nothing more than simple math. *A Winter's Night* was a 500-page book that's being made into a two-hour movie. Melanie is playing the main character, so it shouldn't come as a big surprise that she is in most of the film. On top of that, your brother is on the warpath about wanting this thing wrapped up on time and under budget. That means I don't have time to give every character a fully developed story line. And I certainly don't have time to stop every ten minutes so some idiot can yell at me.

CECELIA Interesting.

BARRY That's one word for it I suppose. Annoying, meddlesome, irksome also work.

CECELIA Are we talking about Janice now or my brother?

BARRY (smiling) What do you think?

MANDY (standing) Well, I'd best be off and find Christina. Thanks for the interview Mr. Meagher. It was nice to see you again, Mrs. Meagher.

Mandy walks away. Barry resumes reading his script. Cecelia glances at Mandy's retreating form and then back at Barry.

CECELIA She seems nice.

BARRY (distracted) Hmmm? Who? Oh, Mandy? Yeah, she's a nice kid. She's just starting out at HNS. She's been assigned to cover "all the scintillating, behind-the-scenes goings on" of our movie. Or at least

I think that's what her editor called it.

CECELIA Be careful, Barry.

BARRY (looking up) Be careful about what? Mandy?

CECELIA Yes. First of all, she's not a kid. And second, she strikes me as someone who doesn't stop digging until they get to the truth. And you and I both know that could be a major problem.

BARRY (looking in the direction of where Mandy just left) I see your point. I'll keep that in mind.

CECELIA Do that. Remember, this doesn't just affect you. It affects all of us.

Thirty-Five

Once we were back in the car, Nigel turned to me. "Why would Mandy want those tapes?" he asked.

"I have a pretty good idea."

"Anything you feel like sharing?" he asked, as he gunned the engine.

"Not until I'm sure," I answered. "Besides, you know the rules. A good detective doesn't reveal her theories until there's proof."

"Much to the everlasting annoyance of their assistants. Honestly, it's a wonder that some of them didn't off their employers. If I were Hastings I would have trashed Poirot with my umbrella."

"I'll make a note to hide all the umbrellas when we get home," I said, as I pulled out my cell phone.

"Who are you calling?" he asked.

"Mandy, of course," I replied. "I'm going to suggest we spend a little girl time together."

"*I* like girl time," Nigel said as we pulled out onto the highway.

"Yes, dear. I know. That little tidbit is what we might call a well-documented fact. But I think this is a visit that would be better served if just I go," I said. "Besides, you said you wanted to work on Skippy's training."

"Spoil sport," Nigel muttered as Mandy answered the phone.

"Mandy?" I said. "It's Nic. Listen, are you busy tomorrow? Nigel is spending the day trying to train Skippy. I thought maybe we could meet for a drink. My treat."

THIRTY-SIX

Mandy agreed, and the next day found us sipping cocktails on a restaurant patio overlooking the ocean. "So, anything new on your break-in?" she asked.

I shrugged. "Oh, a few things," I said.

She turned to me, her expression curious. "Anything you feel like sharing?" she asked.

I shook my head. "Not really. I just want to talk, actually. That's why I called you. I need a little girl time. You know, talk about clothes, gossip, and our love lives."

Mandy laughed. "Well, I can certainly help you with the first two. Unfortunately, I've got nothing for the last one."

I looked at her in surprise. "Really? How come? You're smart, gorgeous, and successful. You're not dating anybody?"

Mandy shrugged. "I date a little, but in my job it's hard to find time for a relationship. I mean a long-term one anyway."

"Really? There's never been anyone? No

one special?"

"Well, I wouldn't say that," she said with a coy smile, "but I guess I'm married to my career. I absolutely love what I do. Even the jobs that involve juice cleanses. I guess I never met the right guy."

"Oh. For some reason, I was under the impression that you had met the right guy."

Mandy adopted a confused expression. "What are you talking about?"

"I'm talking about Barry."

"Barry?" she repeated slowly.

"Barry," I confirmed.

She blanched. "You think I'm in love with Barry?" she asked aghast.

"Well, aren't you?"

She stared at me a beat and then said, "Why on earth would you think that?"

"I've seen the videos, Mandy. I've also seen the way you act around him. I thought it was odd how upset you got at Barry's party when that woman said Barry liked to play around. But, I guess it really fell into place when I talked to Mr. Luiz."

"Who?"

"The actor you hired to try and buy the tapes from us."

"Oh, shit," she said looking at her lap.

I sighed. "Really, Mandy? Barry Meagher? He's married, for God's sake!"

She glared at me. "Don't you think I know that?"

"I know you know it," I retorted. "My question is why?"

She paused and looked out over the ocean before answering. "Our relationship is . . . complicated," she finally said.

I scoffed. "Is that a fancy term for 'sleeping with a married man' "?

"Look, Nic. What do you want me to say? I'm sorry?"

"Why don't you try explaining to me what the hell you were thinking in hiring an actor to buy the tapes from us?"

"I don't know," Mandy said and took a deep drink from her wine glass. "I was pretty sure there was nothing on them. I mean, we were always careful, but I couldn't be sure. I remember meeting him on the set and feeling like I'd been hit with a lightning bolt. I'm sure it was written all over my face. If Cecelia ever found out . . . well, it would be horrible."

"Do you really think that I'd publish anything like that? Why would I do that? We're friends! Your relationship with Barry has nothing to do with how this movie was made! Why didn't you just tell me?"

"Because I was ashamed. It's all such a stupid cliché; the long-time mistress of the powerful man. She happily accepts whatever crumbs of affection he throws her way. She arranges her life for his convenience. God, I make fun of women like me!"

I stared at her. After a moment I said, "You're really in love with him, aren't you?"

She hung her head. "God help me, I am."

Thirty-Seven

Later, as I pulled into our driveway, a squad car rolled up behind me. Glancing in the rearview mirror, I saw that it contained Detective Brady and Officer Hax. Both looked very grim.

I got out of my car, just as Nigel opened the front door. Skippy bounded over to me and greeted me in his usual fashion. By the time I had finished wiping off my face, Detective Brady and Officer Hax had alighted from the car.

"I've been trying to reach you," I said to Detective Brady by way of a greeting. "I have some information that may help with this case."

Detective Brady slammed his car door shut with a decided thud. "Do you, now?" he asked with a faint smirk. "How lucky for me. I can hardly wait to hear it."

I glanced at Officer Hax. While her face was arranged in a professionally blank mask,

I detected annoyance beneath its surface. I shrugged and crossed my arms, leaning against my car door. Nigel walked across the graveled driveway to where I stood. Skippy promptly sat down in front of us.

"I taught him that today," Nigel said as he greeted me with a light kiss on my check.

"I hate to break this to you, darling," I said, "but Skippy has been sitting on his own for some time now."

"Don't be a smartass, I meant in a guarding position," he said. Turning to Detective Brady, he asked, "How can we help you, Detective?"

Detective Brady mirrored my position, crossing his arms and leaning against his car door. "Oh, but by all means," he said with a deliberate drawl, "why don't you tell me your information first? I'm sure it's *far* more important than what I have."

Officer Hax winced at his rudeness. I took a deep breath and let out a sigh. I had dealt with men like Brady long enough that I was now immune to the behavior. In time, Officer Hax would become so too. But for now, she stared intently at her shoes. Without preamble, I told Detective Brady my theory about Melanie's pregnancy and that her death was the result of an intentionally tampered with EpiPen. While I didn't expect him to believe me, I certainly didn't expect him to laugh.

"I'm sorry, Mrs. Martini," he said, "but I've got bigger things to worry about right now than a suspected pregnancy from almost twenty years ago and an allergy to shellfish."

"Such as?" I asked.

The smirk returned. "Well, for starters, the body of Janice Franklin was found early this morning."

"Homicide?" I asked.

Detective Brady gave a slight nod. "We can't be sure yet, of course, until we finish running some more tests. But I've been doing this a long time, and my gut tells me she was murdered."

"What happened?" I asked.

"The victim's daughter, Christina Franklin, had been unable to reach her mother and grew concerned. She went to the victim's house and using her key, let herself inside. There she discovered her mother. The victim had been shot twice in the back."

"Wow," said Nigel with wide-eyed admiration. "That's some gut."

After Officer Hax's sudden coughing fit subsided, I asked if there were any suspects. I was rewarded with a smug smile. "As a matter of fact, there is one. And I'm happy to say that not only do we have them in custody, but I believe that they are also responsible for the attack on your employee."

That did surprise me. "Who?"

"Jules Dixon," came the reply.

That surprised me even more.

THIRTY-EIGHT

"Why don't you come inside?" I suggested. "I'd rather not have this conversation in my driveway."

Detective Brady gave a reluctant nod. "Fine, but I only have a few minutes," he said.

"Of course," I said. "I understand."

I led the way inside to the kitchen. Once everyone was seated and offers of coffee had been politely refused, I sat back in my chair. "So, tell me why you think Jules was behind all of this," I asked.

"There are several reasons, actually," Detective Brady answered as he crossed his legs and brushed a spec of lint off of his pant leg. "But I'll narrow it down to two. First, we have several witnesses who saw an altercation between Ms. Dixon and Ms. Franklin that ended with Ms. Dixon threatening Ms. Franklin. And second, the remains of some of your stolen tapes were found on the grounds of Ms. Dixon's home. It appears that they'd been burned."

"Just to clarify, this would be the house she shares with John Cummings?" I asked.

Detective Brady tipped his head in acknowledgement. "Yes; however, I don't think he's involved. He wasn't in residence at the time of the search."

"Oh, well," I said nodding, "Then that *definitely* clears him."

Detective Brady raised an eyebrow. "Are you being ironic, Ms. Martini?" he asked.

"Technically, I was being sarcastic," I said, "but I don't really want to get into a semantic argument with you. Instead, why don't you just tell me why you think Jules Dixon broke into our house and stole our tapes?"

Detective Brady cocked an eyebrow in my direction. "You really have to ask?" he said. "I would think that as a former detective, you'd be able to figure that out for yourself."

I smiled. "Consider it an early Christmas gift."

Detective Brady re-crossed his legs and made sure they were lint free before continuing. "From what I understand, there has been a lot of interest in those tapes. No doubt, Ms. Dixon thought that if she could acquire them, she could sell them. She may have also planned to use them as a leveraging tool."

"A leveraging tool for what?" I asked.

"Movie roles," he answered. "I understand that Ms. Dixon was up for a movie role; a role for which Ms. Christina Franklin was also being considered. Ms. Dixon may have believed that having these tapes would give her an edge."

I leaned forward, resting my elbows on my knees, and considered his answer. "So, you think that a woman, who by all accounts is quite well off, would resort to savagely beating a person and leaving them for dead just for the chance to make a little money?" I asked after a moment.

Detective Brady shrugged. "Why do you assume it would be a little money?" he asked.

"Ok, let's say the tapes are worth a lot of money. There still is the question as to why a woman, who is already well off, would resort to such savagery."

"You never heard of someone killing for money? Even the rich want to be richer," he asked with a smirk. "You did say you used to work in New York City, correct? I know there's been a big push to reduce crime there in recent years, but I can't image it's suddenly Mayberry."

"Oh, no, there's still plenty of crime. Trust

me, I've seen *more* than my fair share of the baser side of humanity, Detective Brady," I said.

"But you don't think Jules Dixon is a member of this baser side?"

I shook my head. "I never said that. In fact, I think she is a rather unpleasant woman all together. I can easily picture her doing a lot of despicable things. I'm just not sure that attempted murder is one of them."

"Well, I'll be sure to include that observation in my report right under the heading of 'Woman's Intuition,' " Detective Brady said. "And, just so I understand your reasoning, despite the fact that we found some of the stolen videos on her property, you don't think she was behind the theft because . . . why?"

"Actually, it's that fact that the videos were found on her property that bothers me," I said.

Detective Brady frowned. "*That's* what bothers you?"

Before I could answer, Nigel gently stepped on my foot. I amended my initial response. "According to your theory, Jules stole our tapes and almost killed someone in the process because the tapes were extremely valuable and because she — for whatever reason — needed the money."

Detective Brady nodded as if bored.

"Well, I guess my first question would be, if these tapes were so valuable, then why would she burn them?"

Detective Brady rotated his shoulder as if stretching out a sore muscle, before answering. "Maybe she panicked. Realized that we were closing in on her and wanted to destroy the evidence," he finally offered.

I leaned back against the cushions and stared at him a beat before glancing at Officer Hax. She studiously avoided my gaze. I didn't blame her. I'd worked with higher-ups like Brady before too.

Thirty-Nine

As Nigel and I watched Detective Brady and Officer Hax pull out of our driveway, Nigel whispered into my ear, "I don't think Detective Brady likes you."

"I'd be offended if he did."

"I wonder if his gut has told him that we think he's an idiot?" he asked as he made a production of cheerily waving good-bye.

"Impossible," I answered, as I did the same. "That would mean he *had* a gut, and he's clearly all *ass.*"

"You know what this means, though, don't you?" he asked.

"You want to marry me and take me away from all of this?" I suggested.

He smiled down at me. "I believe I already did that."

"You could always do it again," I offered. "But *this* time we could have an Elvis impersonator officiate. That's a Christmas card picture that's just begging to be sent to your family."

"You've got yourself a deal," Nigel said. "I'll make all the arrangements right after you solve this case, which you are on as of now. Because, let's face it, Fred from *Scooby-Doo* had more brains than Detective Brady."

I turned and wrapped my arms around his neck. "Nigel, *Scooby* had more going on than Detective Brady."

Nigel pulled me closer and kissed me lightly on my nose, but his expression was serious. "Exactly," he said, "which is why you need to find who *really* did this to DeDee. She's lying in a hospital bed with no memory all because of those damn tapes."

I leaned back, my arms still around his neck, and met his gaze. "Well, I think I have some good news for you then," I said. "I think I know who did it."

Nigel cocked his head. "You think?"

I nodded. "I just need to make a quick phone call first."

FORTY

Sara Taylor picked up on the first ring. I think she was expecting a call from someone else, if the frustration in her voice when I identified myself was any indication.

"Sara, I'm sorry to bother you," I said, "I know you must be very busy."

"I am," she agreed.

After a brief silent acknowledgement of that lie, I continued. "Yes, well I do appreciate your taking the time to talk to me. I won't be long."

Sara sighed heavily into the phone. "What is it?" she asked

"It's about Melanie's pregnancy," I said.

I heard the intake of breath. "Her . . . what?" she stammered.

"Her pregnancy," I repeated.

"I'm having trouble hearing you," she said. "We must have a bad connection."

"If it's easy, I could come out and talk to you in person."

Sara was silent for a minute and then said, "No, that's all right. I can hear you now."

"Oh, good," I said, "I had a feeling that the connection might improve. Now, I won't keep you long. I already know who the father was but I need you to tell me who was paying you to keep quiet about Melanie's pregnancy."

Silence answered. "Sara?" I began.

She whispered the name so softly that I had to ask her to repeat it to be sure I heard her correctly. Once she did, it all made sense. After a moment Sara asked in a small voice, "What are you going to do?"

"Well, Sara, you'll have to forgive me if I don't go into all the details with you now, but I will tell you this." I paused and let the silence grow.

"Tell me what?" she asked after a minute.

"I think you'd better find a job. Immediately. I have a feeling that your wise investments are about to crash and burn."

I hung up and made one more call. This time it was to Officer Hax.

Forty-One

A few hours later, I knocked on Frank Samuel's front door. Per my request, Officer Hax was parked around the corner in her squad car. Per my request that Nigel and Skippy stay at home, I was less successful. Both of them flanked me as I stood on Frank's doorstep.

Frank answered my knock, his eyes going round with surprise at the sight of us. He quickly recovered and said, "Well, hello, Nic. Hello, Nigel. To what do I owe the pleasure?"

"Hello, Frank," I said apologetically. "I'm sorry to show up unannounced like this, but I need to speak to you about a few things. Is now a convenient time?"

Frank blinked twice and then produced a gracious smile. Taking a step back, he opened the door wide to admit us. "Of course," he said, "please, come in. What seems to be the trouble?"

"Is there somewhere we can talk privately?" I asked.

"I hope you don't mind that we brought Skippy, here," Nigel said. "We're still training him, and he gets upset if we leave him alone."

Frank's smiled wavered briefly, but he nodded and said, "Of course not. No problem at all. Why don't we talk in my study?"

I returned his smile. "Perfect."

Frank led us down a hallway and then into a handsomely furnished room at the back of the house. Large glass windows overlooked a sprawling backyard. The bright blue water of a lap pool was the only other color in a sea of plush green. Frank took a seat at the large mahogany desk while Nigel and I sat in the matching Windsor chairs opposite. Skippy sat between us and stared at Frank.

Placing his elbows on the desk and pressing the tips of his fingers together, Frank regarded us with a genial expression. "Can I offer you something to drink?" he asked. "I've just acquired a 1926 Macallan. I hear you're a man who appreciates a good glass of scotch, Nigel. Can I tempt you?"

"You can do more than that with a '26 Macallan," Nigel said.

Frank laughed and stood up from his

desk. "Good man," he said with an approving nod. "Nic? How about you? Can I make you a drink?"

"Yes, please," I answered. "You don't marry a scotch man without learning to appreciate the drink."

"That is true," Frank said, as he moved to a wet bar off to one side of the room. He poured out the drinks and we all clinked glasses before taking a sip. I wasn't actually a huge fan of scotch, but I knew enough about it to know that this was a superior blend.

Frank sat back down at his desk just as a voice called out, "Dad? Did I hear someone at the front door?" A second later, Danielle's dark head poked around the open doorframe. Seeing us, she produced a friendly smile. "Well, hello, Mr. and Mrs. Martini," she said. "How are you?" Seeing Skippy, her eyes widened. "And who is this?" she asked.

"This is Skippy," Nigel answered.

"Well hello, Skippy," Danielle said.

Skippy cocked his head to one side and wagged his tail as he stared at Danielle. Nigel nudged him with his foot. "Skippy, don't be rude. Say hello."

Skippy barked and offered Danielle his paw. Danielle politely shook it and said, "It's very nice to meet you Skippy."

I glanced at Nigel, an eyebrow raised. He affected a look of modesty — failed miserably — and mouthed the word "training" at me. I rolled my eyes.

"Well, I'll let you get back to your talk," said Danielle. "It was nice to see you again." She gave us a little wave and ducked back out into the hallway.

"You too," Nigel and I called after her.

We looked to Frank. His elbows were once again propped on his desk; fingers pressed together. "So what's this all about?" he asked.

"There is no polite way to put this," I said, "so I'm just going to come right out and say it." Frank raised his eyebrows expectantly. I took a deep breath. "It's about the murder of Janice Franklin."

Frank's eyebrows pulled together in confusion. "I don't understand," he began.

"With all due respect, I think you do. I think you killed Janice because she figured out that it was you who broke into our house, attacked our employee, and stole our tapes."

Frank's hands landed with a thud on the table. "Why the hell would I do that?" he sputtered.

"Because you overheard Nigel at the Vanity Fair Party. You knew that our assistant had seen something on those tapes, something that you didn't want anyone to see. Ever."

Some of Frank's confidence returned. He pressed his fingers together again. "That's ridiculous!" he scoffed. "What on earth could possibly be on those tapes that I'd care about?"

I finished my drink before I answered. It seemed bad form to linger over a man's expensive scotch while you accused him of murder. "How about the fact that Melanie Summers was pregnant with your child?" I asked.

This time his hands went to the desk and stayed there. He blinked hard and then said, "That's absurd."

"Personally, I would call it obscene, but that's neither here nor there," I said. "You were a married man, twenty years her senior, and she was a vulnerable girl," I continued, raising my voice.

Frank scoffed at that. "Melanie was many things, but vulnerable wasn't one of them. She was hard as nails."

"I guess the pregnancy changed that," I said. "She wanted to keep the baby, didn't she? She wanted you to leave Zelda and marry her. From the sounds of it, it seems she thought that was the plan all along. Remember, Frank. I've seen the remaining tapes, you didn't destroy *all* of them."

Frank shifted his eyes from mine. "I never promised her . . ." he began.

"She seemed to think you did," I said. "She got pretty angry when she realized it wasn't true. Is that when you decided to kill her?"

Frank rested his face in his hands, his face pale beneath his deep tan. "I didn't . . ." he started and then abruptly stopped. A thought seemed to occur to him. From the groan that accompanied it, it appeared to be an unwelcome one.

I cut him off. "I talked to Sara Taylor, you know. She told me everything. Sounds like you paid her a pretty penny to stay quiet about Melanie's pregnancy. Still, it's not as much as Melanie had to pay, is it?" Frank said nothing. I pressed on, my voice getting louder and louder. "All this time, her death was listed as another tragic celebrity overdose; a cautionary tale to warn kids about the dangers of drugs. When, in reality, it was something far more insidious. A young woman was taken advantage of by an older, powerful man, and then killed when she became a threat to his reputation."

Frank remained silent, his head still in his

hands. I stood up. "You overhead Nigel on the phone with DeDee at the Vanity Fair Party. You knew she was trying to tell him that Melanie's EpiPen had been tampered with. You couldn't let that information get out, could you? You had to get those tapes. And you did." I took a deep breath. Nigel nodded at me to continue. "But I guess after twenty years, your luck ran out and Janice called in the debt. I'm guessing that she knew what you did, but she wasn't interested in justice. She was only interested in making sure Christina was cast in your new movie. What happened, Frank? Did she see the picture of you and Barry leaving the Vanity Fair Party? The one with you holding your Oscar? Did she realize that you couldn't have had your Oscar because you'd given it to Danielle to take home? Is that what happened?" I was yelling now, frustrated at his lack of response. Without a confession, I had very little proof. After a few seconds, I was rewarded with one.

"You almost had it right," came the answer. The tension in my neck began to ease. Right until I turned around and saw the gun.

Forty-Two

"Danielle! What the hell are you doing?" Frank yelled jumping to his feet.

"It wasn't him. It was me," Danielle said in a small voice. She was standing in the doorway, the gun in her hand trained on my chest. Nigel shifted in his chair. Danielle briefly glanced his way. "Stay right there," she said, her voice wavering slightly. "I don't want to have to hurt your dog, but I will if I have to."

Nigel caught my eye, and I gave a nod. "Is that the gun you used to kill Janice?" I asked.

Danielle studied me a moment before nodding. "It is," she said.

"Danny! No!" cried Frank in horror. "What are you saying?"

"I shot Janice," Danielle said in a soft voice. She looked at Frank, her eyes pleading for understanding. "She was a horrible woman. She was an even worse mother."

"You don't know what you're saying, Danny," Frank said, his voice a hoarse whisper. "I can help you, but not if you keep talking."

"Janice came here looking for you the other night," she continued as if he hadn't spoken. "The night you were at that dinner. I could tell she was upset about something. I said that I didn't know when you were coming back, but she insisted on waiting. I let her wait in the study. She must have waited about two hours." Danielle looked at Frank. "Before she left, she gave me a letter to give to you. She said that it was vital that you read it as soon as you got home. I read it instead." Danielle paused and squeezed her eyes shut. "She'd seen the picture in the paper of you leaving the party with your Oscar. She'd seen me leave earlier with one, too." Danielle opened her eyes and looked at Frank. "But Janice had it backward. She assumed that you were behind the attack. She said she'd keep quiet as long as you gave Christina that role. But I knew she wouldn't stop there. Women like Janice never stop. They have to *be* stopped."

I folded my arms over my chest. "Is that why you killed Melanie?" I asked. "Did she need to be stopped, too?"

Anger flared in Danielle's eyes. "Melanie

was about to ruin my life," she said. "I couldn't let her do that. If my mom found out about the pregnancy, she would have filed for divorce. I knew what that would mean. Everything would be ripped apart. I'd grow up being shuttled back and forth between homes just like most of my friends. Except in my case, my homes would be in two different countries."

"And yet that's what happened anyway," I said, not unkindly.

Danielle blew out a long breath. "Yeah. But, I didn't know that *then. Then,* I just wanted to prevent it. I just wanted to save my parents' marriage. I just wanted to save my life."

I cocked an eyebrow at her. "Even if it meant taking someone else's?"

Danielle stared at me, her eyes blank. "She was going to ruin everything. Don't you get it? She had to go." She looked at Frank. "You understand, don't you, Daddy? I didn't want to lose you. I couldn't lose *you.* She had to go." In a firmer voice, she repeated, "Melanie *had* to go. There was no other way."

Frank sank into his chair with a half sob. "Oh, my God," he moaned as he covered his face with his hands, "Oh, my God. Danny. Danny, why?"

Danielle stared at him incredulous. "Why? *Why?* I did it so I could be with *you.* You always said I was your special little girl. I couldn't let someone take that away from me." Danielle's voice broke. "Daddy?" she pleaded, "Tell me you understand."

Frank didn't answer. He was caught up in his own misery. "Zelda said something to me once. She said to watch you. I didn't listen to her. I thought she was being silly. . . ."

Danielle's focus remained fixed on Frank's hidden face. Nigel eased himself out of the chair and began to edge his way toward me.

After a minute, a haunted expression came over Danielle's face. "Daddy," she said, her voice pleaded, "I can fix this. I'll fix this and then we can start over. You'll see. It'll be fine."

I glanced at Nigel just as Danielle turned toward me and aimed the gun at my chest. Everything seemed to happen at once. The gun went off. Nigel yelled, "Rosebud!" and dove for me. Skippy lunged at Danielle. Officer Hax rounded the corner, her gun drawn and screamed, "Freeze!"

Then there was a loud crack as my head hit the floor and things went black.

Forty-Three

When I opened my eyes again, Danielle lay sprawled on her back. Skippy sat squarely on her chest, a low growl coming from his throat warning her not to move. Based on her incoherent sobs, it didn't seem like something we needed to worry about. Frank was on the phone with 911. Officer Hax had her gun trained on Danielle, while she too called for backup and an ambulance. I wondered why we needed the latter until I looked down to see my sweater covered in blood. Nigel saw it too. "Don't worry. You're going to be fine," he kept repeating, his face pale, as he gently patted me trying to find the source of the bleeding.

"Nigel, I'm okay," I said looking up into worried eyes.

"Of course, you are," he said with an encouraging smile. "I'm sure it's just a scratch."

I struggled to sit up. "Nigel," I tried again.

"*I'm* okay. I wasn't hit. *You* were."

Nigel stared at me in confusion. "But, I don't feel . . ." he began.

"You will," I said, as I yanked off my sweater and gently pressed it against the gaping hole in his shoulder.

His face went a little paler as he looked down at his arm. "Oh," he said.

I sat him up against the wall, keeping the pressure firm. "You okay?" I asked.

He nodded grimly. "Never liked this shirt anyway."

I looked over at Officer Hax. "Did you get it all?" I asked.

She nodded and tapped her phone. "Loud and clear," she said. "It recorded perfectly." She glanced at Nigel. "Ambulance is on its way."

I looked back to Nigel. His mouth was pinched in pain. "I'm fine," he said. He glanced over at Skippy. "Did you see what he did?" he asked. "The way he tackled her? I taught him that."

"I saw. Did I imagine it, or did I hear you yell, 'Rosebud'?" I asked.

"You didn't imagine it. That's his attack word."

"Wasn't that done on an episode of *Columbo*?" I asked.

Nigel gave me a weak smile. "I love the

fact that you know that."

Officer Hax gave a low cough. We both looked over to her. "Um, speaking of your dog," she said with a nod to Skippy, who was still sitting on Danielle. "Should we get him off of her?"

Nigel shrugged. "I don't know. He looks comfortable to me."

Forty-Four

A few hours later, the doctors had dug out the bullet and patched up Nigel's shoulder. His face now wore a tranquil expression that I assumed was from the morphine as the nurse had denied his request for a martini.

My own expression was far less serene. So, too was my mood. In my defense, I was dealing with a seemingly never-ending series of questions from Detective Brady. He was irate. I wondered if I could get a morphine drip too.

"So, would you care to explain to me how Officer Hax just happened to record the Samuels girl's confession?" he asked scornfully.

"I must have dialed her by accident," I lied. "It was a little chaotic in there." I saw no point in telling Detective Brady that I had called Officer Hax and arranged everything in advance. As soon as I got Danielle talking, Nigel hit the record button on his phone while I hit the call button on mine. Officer Hax could then listen and come in when needed. It was just too bad she wasn't a minute sooner.

"So, your story is that you butt dialed Officer Hax? During a killer's confession no less?" he asked, his face turning red.

"I can't think of any other reason," I said. "Thank God she was in the neighborhood and got there in time. She's an excellent officer. I hope she gets recognized for her bravery today."

That earned me a glare. "I don't like to find out people are doing things behind my back," he said.

"Then I'd make it a habit not to turn around," advised Nigel from behind closed eyes.

Detective Brady looked over to where Nigel lay, propped up in his hospital bed with Skippy curled protectively at his feet. "What the hell do you mean by that?" he snapped. "And what the hell is that dog doing here? He shouldn't be here. This is a hospital."

Skippy raised his massive head and stared at Detective Brady. "Would *you* care to explain that to him?" I asked.

Detective Brady apparently did not. He looked away from Skippy and resumed questioning me. "Let's go over this again," he said. "You were at Frank Samuels's house because . . . why?"

I sighed and repeated what I'd already said five times now. "I realized that Melanie Summers was pregnant with Frank's child when she died. DeDee must have seen something on the tapes that led her to believe that someone had tampered with Melanie's EpiPen. That's what she was trying to tell us the night she was attacked. I believe I told *you* this, but you didn't seem to think it was important."

Detective Brady motioned for me to hurry over that part of the narrative. "That's neither here nor there now," he said. "According to Mr. Samuels's statement, you first accused *him* of the crimes."

I nodded. "A bluff, if you will. I really didn't have any concrete proof it was Danielle. I gambled that if she heard me accuse her father, she'd try and protect him. And it worked."

Detective Brady blinked. Twice. "So, if you had no proof, what made you think it was her?" he asked.

"At one point on the footage, Melanie holds up a cup of pudding and says, 'I'm in the club!' I didn't know until Nigel told me, but 'In the pudding club' is a slang term for being pregnant. It struck me as odd that Frank didn't comment on Melanie's remark. Until I remembered that Frank went to Harvard too. If he was familiar with the term, there was a good chance that his daughter might be as well. A nearby glass window caught her reflection as she filmed. She appears stunned and then furious. The day before that, Melanie had an argument with someone in her trailer. It's not clear who she's talking to, but it is clear that Melanie is furious. When you listen to the fight with the knowledge that Melanie is pregnant, it suddenly makes sense. Melanie was threatening to tell the world that Frank was the father of her baby. Danielle knew that and panicked. She knew that would ruin her parent's marriage." I paused. "But it wasn't until Janice's death that it started to make any sense. I had seen Janice react oddly to the paper's coverage of the Oscars when I had lunch with Christina. I had seen the same paper. At first I didn't see anything odd, but then I looked again. There's a picture of Frank and Barry holding their Oscars as they leave the Vanity Fair Party. But earlier I'd seen Danielle leaving with a statue. I imagine Janice did, too. She realized that someone went home with Christina's Oscar and tried to use that information to force Frank into giving Christina a role in *The Deposition.* Except Janice had it backward. Frank didn't take Christina's Oscar. Danielle did."

Detective Brady's mouth hung open for a beat and then snapped shut. It was a good look on him.

Forty-Five

The hospital discharged Nigel the next day. His arm was in a sling and would be for the next several weeks. He grumbled about it, but I knew he was secretly pleased. Whenever anybody would ask him about it, he'd give a wry laugh, and say, "What, this? Oh, it's nothing, really. Certainly not heroic. The papers made it out to be more than it was."

I didn't begrudge him of it one bit. After all, the man had taken a bullet for me.

A few days after he'd been home, Mandy came to visit us. With her she brought a large bouquet of flowers, a large bottle of scotch, and an even larger dog bone. "You can distribute these however you see fit," she said as she thrust them all into my arms. "I've been a horrible friend, and I'm sorry."

"There's no need to apologize," I assured her. By mutual agreement we avoided the topic of Barry. Mandy was a grown woman. It wasn't my place to tell her that she was an idiot. Besides, on some level, I think she already knew. "Come out back and see Nigel," I said. "He's stoically lounging by the pool."

Mandy followed me out to where Nigel lay on the chaise. "You look quite dashing with the sling," she said as she sat in the chair next to him. "Getting shot seems to agree with you."

He grinned. "Well, I don't recommend it for everyone, obviously," he said. "But I've tried to make the best of it."

"Don't encourage him, Mandy," I warned. "He's close to becoming insufferable."

Nigel pretended to glare at me. "I took a bullet for you, woman! Show some gratitude!"

"I'm sorry. Do you want me to go put on the nurse's uniform again?" I asked sweetly.

Mandy groaned. "If you do, I'm leaving."

I laughed. "Sorry. So, what's going on in your world?" I asked her. "We've kind of had our heads buried here. We did get some good news though. DeDee's sister called. Her memory has started to return. She doesn't remember everything yet, but she was able to give the police a statement fingering Danielle as her attacker. Her doctors say that she's going to be fine."

"I'm glad to hear it," she said. Shaking

her head, she added, "I still can't believe that Danielle killed Melanie all those years ago. Frank's having a hard time dealing with it, too. He's gone off on some six-week zen retreat that forbids outside communication."

"How nice for him," I said. It still made my stomach churn to think about Frank. He'd taken advantage of a troubled young woman and then had been ready to toss her aside when she got pregnant. Granted, he hadn't killed her, but that didn't mean he was innocent. I wondered how many other Melanies had been callously used by men like Frank over the years. Then I realized I didn't want to know the answer. I suspected it would be heartbreaking. "How is Christina doing?" I asked to change the subject.

"Good, actually," said Mandy. "She's moving on, just as she always has. She hired Sebastian as her manager. I think they'll work well with each other. But the really big new is that John left Jules." Mandy's eyes danced with amusement.

I glanced up in surprise. "Really?"

She nodded. "Yup. But that's not the best part. John went back to Christina and begged her to take him back. Got down on his knees and everything. In a crowded restaurant, no less."

"And did she? Take him back?"

Mandy shook her head, her smile broadening. "She did *not.* She told him in no uncertain terms that he was a low-down dirty dog and that she wanted nothing more to do with him. It was perfect. I told you her Oscar speech was all an act. And a damn good one, too."

"This is a strange town, Mandy," I said after a minute.

Mandy sighed in agreement. "You have no idea, Nic," she said. "No idea."

After Mandy left, Nigel and I sat by the water and quietly sipped our drinks. Skippy lay sprawled out on a pool raft, lightly dozing in the afternoon sun.

"I've been thinking," Nigel said after a while.

"About?"

"That maybe we need to go on a vacation," he said. "Expose Skippy to a little culture."

I studied him over the rim of my drink glass. "Any place in particular?" I asked.

"Well, I did hear about this one beach in Italy," he said with a smile. "I've made reservations. All that's waiting is your approval to book them."

"Do they serve dirty martinis there?"

"They do indeed."

I leaned back and closed my eyes against the afternoon sun. “Then, in the immortal words of Steve McGarrett, ‘Book ’em, Danno. Book ’em.’ ”

FOOTAGE FROM THE SET OF *A WINTER'S NIGHT* 5/8/96

Frank and Zelda are sitting in an empty stage set designed as a 1940s nightclub. They are eating a homemade lunch from a picnic basket. They are not speaking and appear tense.

ZELDA Have you talked to her yet?
FRANK No.
ZELDA Something's wrong.
FRANK (shaking his head) Nothing is wrong! You worry too much.
ZELDA (watches him as she takes a bit of her sandwich) And you don't worry enough.
FRANK (looking up) What is that supposed to mean?
ZELDA It means that you never think anything bad can touch you. It's childish. There is good and bad in this world, Frank. We all get an equal amount.
FRANK Yes, but . . .

ZELDA I mean it Frank. I'm worried. There's something going on with her. A mother knows these things.

Camera shuts off.

RECIPES

The Oscar

Ingredients:

75 ml (2 1/2 oz.) Plymouth gin
Juice from 1/2 pink grapefruit
25 ml (3/4 oz.) of elderflower syrup
1 rosemary sprig

The Diva

Ingredients:

90 ml (3 oz.) vodka
45 ml (1 1/2 oz.) pineapple juice
15 ml (1/2 oz.) kiwi syrup
Mint leaves for garnish

The Red Carpet

Ingredients:

70 ml (2 1/2 oz.) vodka
30 ml (1 oz.) raspberry liquor
20 ml (3/4 oz.) raspberry syrup
40 ml (1 1/2 oz.) fresh raspberry juice

The Best Boy

Ingredients:

10 ml (1/4 oz.) Martini Extra Dry vermouth
50 ml (1 1/2 oz.) Bombay Sapphire gin
15 ml (1/4 oz.) blue curaçao
Twist of orange for garnish

ABOUT THE AUTHOR

Tracy Kiely received a BA in English from Trinity College. This accomplishment prompted most job interviewers to ask, "How fast can you type?" Her standard answer of "not so fast" usually put an end to further questions.

She was eventually hired by the American Urological Association (AUA), who were kind enough to overlook the whole typing thing — mainly because they knew just what kind of prose she'd be typing. After several years, Tracy left the AUA, taking with her a trove of anecdotal stories that could eventually result in her banishment from polite society. That's when she thought writing a novel might be a good idea.

Murder with a Twist was her first novel in the Nic and Nigel Martini series. It can be enjoyed straight up or with a twist. She is also the author of the Jane Austen-inspired Elizabeth Parker mystery series: *Murder at*

Longbourn, Murder on the Bride's Side, Murder Most Persuasive, and *Murder Most Austen.* These can be enjoyed with either tea or a very dry sherry.

Tracy lives in Maryland with her husband and three children.

The employees of Thorndike Press hope you have enjoyed this Large Print book. All our Thorndike, Wheeler, and Kennebec Large Print titles are designed for easy reading, and all our books are made to last. Other Thorndike Press Large Print books are available at your library, through selected bookstores, or directly from us.

For information about titles, please call:
(800) 223-1244

or visit our Web site at:
http://gale.cengage.com/thorndike

To share your comments, please write:

Publisher
Thorndike Press
10 Water St., Suite 310
Waterville, ME 04901